THE
ENCHANTED COIN

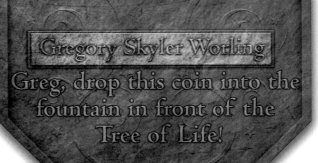

Gregory Skyler Worling

Greg, drop this coin into the
fountain in front of the
Tree of Life!

Bob Doerr

TotalRecall Publications, Inc.
www.totalrecallpress.com

TotalRecall Publications, Inc.
1103 Middlecreek
Friendswood, Texas 77546
281-992-3131   281-482-5390 Fax
www.totalrecallpress.com

Printed in the United States of America with simultaneous printings in Australia, Canada, and United Kingdom.

FIRST EDITION
1   2   3   4   5   6   7   8   9   10

To my girls

Author: Bob Doerr

 grew up in a military family, graduated from the Air Force Academy, and had a twenty eight year career of his own in the Air Force that exposed him to the people and cultures in Asia, Europe and of these United States. Bob specialized in criminal investigations and counterintelligence gaining significant insight to the worlds of crime, espionage and terrorism. His work brought him into close contact and coordination with the FBI and CIA, along with the investigative and security agencies of many different countries. His education credits include a Masters in International Relations from Creighton University.

Now a full time author, Bob has four mystery/thrillers already published and a fifth to be released in the fall. Two of his books, Cold Winter's Kill and Loose Ends Kill, were selected as finalists for the Eric Hoffer Award. Loose Ends Kill was also awarded the 2011 Silver medal for Fiction/mystery by the Military Writers Society of America. Another Colorado Kill and Dead Men Can Kill are winners in the first quarter 2012 beta Ultimate Hero Contest.

Bob lives in Garden Ridge, Texas, with Leigh, his wife of 39 years.

Acknowledgement

"I would like to thank Kaiden Kirby in helping me take this book from concept to reality. I also want to thank Heather Brown for her review and support."

The Book

Gregory's discovery of a magic coin in a pond on his parent's farm takes him on a mystical journey to a strange world, where he encounters prehistoric animals and risks his life to help a young princess save her tribe's lands.

The Enchanted Coin is a fantasy adventure targeted at Middle Grade readers. Imagine being a fourteen year old again and finding a coin that seems to give off a light of its own. The coin has your name on it, and instructs you to toss it into a fountain next to the *Tree of Life*. That's what happens in *The Enchanted Coin*, and what starts my protagonist off on a magical adventure that many young boys and girls would love to have.

This book is "G" rated.

Gregory Worling:
teen age boy and main character who finds the magical coin

Cindy Worling:
Greg's sister, the only person Greg has confided in about the coin

Fawn:
second princess of the Cherakoo, and the person Greg realizes he was sent to this strange world to help and protect

Old Prophet:
an old prophet and friend of Fawn; he helps Greg and Fawn in their mission and helps Greg understand why he may have been sent to this world

Introduction

We have all heard of tales of UFO's, ghosts, of people who say they can talk to the spirits, ancient curses, and of magical talismans. Most of us automatically dismiss them as false, figments of people's imagination, and understandably so. However, might not just a few of them be true? I don't know, but I heard this story from a young man the other day who swore the fascinating tale I have set forth in this book really did occur, because it actually happened to him.

You be the judge.

CHAPTER 1

Greg rolled over in bed and glanced at his bedroom window. The sun shone in through the cracks in the closed blinds. He looked sleepily at the bright slivers of light.

"It's morning!" he realized suddenly and jumped out of bed. Ever since he had discovered the coin, he had been waiting for this day to arrive. He and the rest of his family would board an airplane in a few hours and fly to Orlando, Florida. Once there, they would spend three days at Disney World. He dressed quickly and ran downstairs to the kitchen.

Rebecca Worling, Greg's mother, stood at the stove frying bacon in the old, black iron skillet that she had used as long as Greg could remember.

"Why Gregory, you're up and dressed early this morning," she said.

"Aren't you excited, too, Mom?" Greg asked. He wished his mother would stop calling him Gregory. He much preferred being called Greg. His sister and father referred to him as Greg, but his mother said she had named him Gregory Skyler Worling when he was born, because she liked the name Gregory, and had no intention of calling him anything else.

"Sure I am," his mother answered. "I've never been there either, you know."

"Really?" Greg asked. He found it hard to believe someone as old as his mother, he thought she had turned thirty five last month on her birthday, had never been to Disney World. Rather than answer his question, his mother simply smiled and turned her attention back to the frying bacon.

The smell of the bacon made Greg hungry, but he knew if he asked his mother if he could have a snack while he waited for breakfast, she would tell him to be patient and wait. He heard the television in the family room and realized that his sister, Cindy, must already be awake. He crossed through the kitchen and went into the family room.

"Cindy, are you excited?" Greg asked as he approached her. She had curled up on the couch and had covered herself with a blanket.

"Oh, yes! I couldn't sleep at all last night!"

"Me, too," Greg confessed.

Cindy looked at him conspiratorially. "Are you going to bring the coin?" she whispered.

"Shh!" Greg regretted that he had told Cindy about the coin. It wasn't that he didn't trust his sister. He simply felt that his discovery had been something that was meant just for him. "Remember, Mom and Dad can't know about the coin."

"But why? Why don't you want Mom and Dad to know about the coin?" Cindy asked.

"It's like I said Cindy, I don't know why. It's just that I have this feeling. I'm not sure I should've even told you."

"You know you can trust me. I won't tell anyone."

"I know, Cindy," Greg reached over and touched the tip of her nose with his index finger. It was something he had done since she was a baby, and it had always made her smile. Cindy had had her long brown hair cut really short the day before. He thought to himself that she was growing up faster than he was.

She had even grown to within a few inches of his five foot six.

"Breakfast is ready!   Come and get it!" their mother called from the kitchen.

CHAPTER 2

Greg sat in a window seat on the airplane. Its loud take-off amazed him, and although he would've denied it, the plane's climb into the sky frightened him a little bit, too. For good luck, he had held his breath and counted to ten when the big plane lifted off the runway. One of his friends, Tommy Burke, had told him that he always did that for good luck after making a wish. At the time, Greg thought that holding your breath in order to bring yourself good luck seemed a silly thing to do, but when the airplane's nose lifted up, and he felt the wheels leave the safety of the ground, holding his breath for a count to ten hadn't seemed silly at all.

Now that the plane had leveled off and flew smoothly, miles above the earth, his fear had subsided, and his thoughts turned toward the eight sided coin he had found at the edge of the pond on his parents' small farm. The coin had a shine to it that made it impossible to miss, despite the muddy water that covered it. In fact, he recalled that it was the coin's glow that attracted him to it.

Over the weeks, the glow had faded to the point that he could no longer see any light coming from the coin. The writing on the coin had faded along with its glow, but fortunately Greg had written down the instructions that he had read over and over again the first few days the coin was in his possession.

Greg secretly studied the coin and the small sheet of paper on which he had written down the words inscribed on the coin.

He sat one row behind his parents and Cindy, a position for which he had gladly volunteered. He had said he wanted Cindy and his parents to be together on the flight. While that was true, his primary motivation was his desire to be alone with his coin.

He had compared what he had written on the paper with the small print on the coin a dozen times since he had written them down. Now, even with the use of a magnifying glass, reading the words on the coin was difficult. Every time he double checked the words on the paper he found them an exact match, but even today on the flight he had his doubts. The words on the paper read:

**Greg, drop this coin into the fountain
in front of the Tree of Life!**

**The reverse of the coin also had a strange inscription on it:
Magic Coin 22 of 51**

On that first day of discovery, the letters in the inscriptions had glowed brightly in his hand. When he first saw his own name on the coin, Greg's initial impulse was to toss the coin back into the pond. However, for whatever reason, he stood there as though he were frozen until he came to the realization that for whatever reason the coin held a message intended for him and no one else.

He went home and immediately looked up Tree of Life on the computer, but after researching for nearly an hour and finding a lot of different information on various Trees of Life, Greg still didn't feel any closer to understanding the instructions on the coin. Then it happened! By chance or by magic he didn't know, but that night at dinner his parents announced that the family would be going to Disney World for a vacation as soon as school was out for the summer.

In that instant, Greg remembered that one of the websites he had visited talked about the Tree of Life located at Disney World! His parent's announcement, along with the discovery of the coin, reinforced Greg's belief that the message on the coin had truly been intended for him.

He looked out the airplane's window and wondered what would happen in just a few hours, when he finally stood there in front of the Tree of Life and tossed the coin into the fountain. He felt a sudden sense of dread that frightened him. What if something bad happened?

He looked up and saw Cindy peaking at him from between the seats. He shook his head at her, and she turned around.

"Attention! This is the Captain speaking. Flight attendants, please prepare the cabin for our arrival at Orlando. We will be touching down in just a few minutes."

Greg looked around, unsure what the pilot's instructions meant for him. He heard a flight attendant tell someone nearby to fasten his seatbelt and bring the back of the seat to the upright position. Greg had not taken off his seat belt and had not done anything with the back of his seat, so he simply sat still and waited for the flight attendant to walk by. He guessed that if he needed to do something else, she would tell him.

Sure enough, when she came to the row in the airplane where Greg sat, she leaned in a little and spoke directly to him. As she did, Greg thought the flight attendant looked sort of like Ms. Brooks, one of the teachers at his school.   Except Ms. Brooks didn't have a thin streak of blue running through her otherwise blond hair.

"Gregory," the flight attendant said, "don't forget the Tree of Life."

Greg didn't know what to say. He just nodded and watched as she walked away.

The airplane bounced as it went through some mild turbulence, and, for a few moments, Greg focused his attention on the plane's descent. He didn't know if it had been more frightening at takeoff when they were moving away from the ground, or now during landing as the plane moved closer and closer to it.

Overcoming his fear, Greg made himself watch through the window as the plane descended and finally landed at Orlando International Airport.

"Who're you looking for?" Cindy asked as they walked down the aisle toward the airplane's exit.

"The lady flight attendant, the one who spoke to me just before we landed. You know, the blond one who looks like Ms. Brooks."

"You mean the school teacher? Was she on our airplane?" Cindy asked.

"No, Cindy, she only looked like Ms. Brooks," Greg said.

"I don't remember seeing anyone like that."

Greg looked all around, but he was too short to see past the crowd of adults who were also getting off the airplane. He wanted to ask what she had meant, but he couldn't see her anywhere on the plane.

Only later, while the family drove away from the airport in a rental car did Greg see the flight attendant again. They had only traveled a short distance when his father had to stop the car for a red light. Greg saw her standing nearby, on the sidewalk. She looked directly at him, as though she had been waiting for him, and said the word, "Remember."

Greg didn't actually hear the word, but he saw her lips move and somehow, he just knew that was what she had said, "Remember." He also thought that the ribbon of blue in her hair had become thicker. Greg turned to see if Cindy had also seen the woman, but she had been looking out her own window at a woman in a purple dress walking a poodle wearing a large purple ribbon.

When Greg turned back, he noticed that the flight attendant on the sidewalk had disappeared. The light turned green and Greg's father drove the car out onto the expressway and toward Disney World.

"I won't forget," Greg whispered to himself.

"What did you say?" asked Cindy.

"Oh, nothing, I just can't wait to get there," Greg answered.

CHAPTER 3

"How big is this place?" Greg asked his parents. It hadn't taken them long to reach the entrance to Disney World from the airport, but since passing by the entrance sign they had driven for another ten minutes.

"It's actually quite large," his mother answered. "Your father and I thought it might be interesting to drive around a bit before we went to check into the hotel."

Greg didn't respond to his mother's answer. He had to admit to himself that the size and beauty of the park did impress him, but he also had a mission to accomplish. Until he tossed the coin into the fountain, he knew he wouldn't be able to fully enjoy himself at the park.

"But, Mom," Cindy said, "I can't wait to go on the rides. Can we stop and go on one of the roller coasters?"

"We'll have plenty of time to do a lot of rides. Don't you want to see Mickey Mouse and Goofy, too?"

"Oh, Mom, they're for little kids. I'm nearly eleven," Cindy said. Cindy actually did want to see them, Snow White in particular, but there was no way she was going to admit that to anyone now that she was almost eleven years old.

She looked over at Greg, who smiled at her. She guessed that Greg knew how she really felt about seeing Mickey and the rest of the Disney characters. She had a great relationship with her brother. Greg had always been there to help her and comfort her whenever she got hurt or got into trouble. In fact,

Cindy believed that Greg was the best big brother a girl could have.

A strange feeling had fallen over her since the airplane had landed barely an hour ago. The feeling had grown stronger when they entered the park. Cindy wanted to talk to Greg about it, but she knew she would have to wait until they were out of the car and alone. The feeling frightened her. She felt like a danger sign had started flashing in her mind and she knew it had something to do with Greg's coin. She didn't know what she could do to help her brother, but she vowed to herself she would stay close to him until the coin was safely in that fountain Greg had mentioned.

After a few more minutes of driving they arrived at their hotel. Greg helped his dad take the suitcases up to the large hotel room that consisted of two sleeping areas. His mother had referred to the hotel room as a suite, which she explained was not spelled s-w-e-e-t.

"It's rather late in the afternoon, and your mother and I thought we'd spend the next few hours here at the hotel swimming and exploring the area in and around the hotel. After dinner, we'll head out to watch the fireworks show. They're supposed to be fantastic," their father said.

"Oh!" Cindy moaned. "Can't we go on any rides?"

"Tomorrow we'll get up early and go on all the rides you want all day long," their father said. "Greg will get to pick where we'll spend the day, and then on Sunday, Cindy, it'll be your turn. Monday, your mother and I will pick. How does that sound?"

At first, Greg had wanted to complain like Cindy had done, but his dad had said he could choose the place tomorrow. He could wait that long, he thought. He looked at Cindy hoping she wouldn't say she wanted first choice. She didn't.

"Okay," Greg answered for both of them.

The rest of the day turned out to be so much fun that Greg actually forgot about the coin and its instructions. He loved the hotel's large swimming pool. Greg had learned to swim about the same time he started school, and while he still couldn't beat his dad when they raced from one end of the pool to the other, he was getting closer. When his dad said he was "pooped" and got out of the pool, Greg felt like he still had a lot of energy. He stayed in the water and continued swimming and playing with the other kids in the pool.

"Awesome!" Cindy had said to him later that night as they watched the fireworks show.

"It sure is," he had to agree.

It wasn't until after the family had returned to the hotel for the night that Greg's thoughts finally returned to the coin. He double checked to make sure it was still in the drawer with his clothes before climbing into bed.

He thought he might have a hard time falling asleep, but it seemed that he had barely pulled the covers over him when Cindy was already shaking him to get up.

"Come on, Greg, get up! Mom and Dad are already up," Cindy said.

"What?" Greg asked, as he sat up and rubbed his eyes. "I just got into bed."

"Well, it's morning now. What place are you going to choose?"

"You know. I told you I have to go to Animal Kingdom Park. That's where the Tree of Life is," Greg said.

"I know. It's just that I didn't know if you had changed your mind. I'm getting a little scared," Cindy said.

"Scared? There's no reason for you to be afraid. Everything will be okay, I know it will."

Cindy wondered if everything really would be.

CHAPTER 4

"Well, son, what's your choice for today?" Mr. Worling asked Greg as the family ate breakfast.

"The Animal Kingdom, Dad, and I want to go to see the Tree of Life first."

"Okay, then that's what we'll do," his father said.

"Are you sure the Tree of Life is in the Animal Kingdom?" Greg's mother asked.

"Yes, Mom, I've read a lot about it. It's supposed to be really neat, and there's even a theater in its roots," Greg replied.

"My gosh! I'd like to see that, too," his mother said.

"Me too," added Cindy.

"You have quite the appetite this morning, Greg," his father said. "That's your third pancake, and you already ate all those scrambled eggs and bacon."

"It must have been all that swimming," Greg answered.

When their server brought Greg's parents the bill, Greg took the coin out of his pocket. He wanted to see if it had changed at all, now that he had brought it this close to its destination. It looked the same. He started to put it back in his pocket when his mother's voice stopped him.

"What do you have there, Greg?" she asked.

"Oh, just my lucky coin," he said.

"Can I see it?" she asked.

Greg didn't know what to do. He didn't want to lose the coin, but certainly his mother would give it back to him.

Hesitantly, he held out his hand with the coin in it. His mother took it from him.

"What an interesting shape," she said. "It's certainly not like any coin I've ever seen before. Honey, have you seen a coin like this before?" She held the coin out for Greg's father to inspect.

He took it from her and rolled it over in his hand.

"It has something inscribed on it," his father said. "But it's too small for me to read. On this side, I think I can read something. It says 'Magic', doesn't it, Greg?"

"I think so, Dad," Greg answered. "Can I have it back?"

His father looked at Greg, but did not give him the coin. "Where did you get it?"

"I found it in the pond out in our field." Greg said, resisting the strong urge to ask for the coin again.

"Its shape is peculiar," Mr. Worling said. He rolled the coin around in his hand. "Hmmm, I bet Professor Nettles could tell us if it's a real coin or not. Maybe I'll show it to him."

"Dad, can I have it back, please?" Greg asked.

"Gregory, you know the word is "may," not can. It's may I have the coin back," Greg's mother said. "Dear, give Gregory back his coin."

Mr. Worling hesitated for a moment, almost like he didn't want to let go of the coin, but then he returned it to Greg.

"Thanks, Dad," Greg said, much relieved that he had the coin back in his own hands.

"If I remember right, ancient civilizations believed that an octagon symbolized regeneration and even salvation. A transition to something better, or something like that," Mr. Worling said.

"That means it's a good luck coin, right Dad?" Greg asked.

"I guess so."

The conversation turned to the day ahead and all the things everyone wanted to do. Luckily, his parents didn't change their minds about letting Greg make the final decision. Shortly after breakfast, the family jumped into their rental car and headed to the Animal Kingdom.

"Wow," Greg exclaimed, "look how big the Tree of Life is!"

"Whew," said his mother, "that is certainly a giant tree, by far the biggest I've seen in my entire life."

"Can we go to the theater?" asked Cindy, referring to the theater that was supposed to be located in the trees giant root system.

"Is that okay Gregory?" asked his mother.

"Sure, but let's spend just a few minutes looking at the tree from the outside."

Greg frowned with worry. He hadn't seen a fountain anywhere around the front of the tree. He wanted to pull out the piece of paper on which he had copied the instructions to see if he had forgotten some clue. But he knew he hadn't. He had memorized those instructions.

"Mom, do you mind if I just take a quick look around that side of the tree?" He pointed toward the one side of the tree he hadn't seen. It didn't look like there was a fountain hidden over there, but it was a huge tree. One side of the tree bordered the lake. They walked by another side before arriving here at the front of the tree, and he hadn't seen a fountain anywhere.

"Sure," his mother answered, "but you can see most of that side from here. Go ahead. We'll just sit on this bench until you get back."

"Yes, Greg, go ahead. Your mother and I will sit here," Mr.

Worling said in agreement.

"I'll go with you," said Cindy, and she followed Greg as he walked away. Although she didn't say anything to her brother, Cindy felt an uncomfortable urgency to stay close to her brother's side.

They had to follow the sidewalk away from the tree for a few yards, before they could turn right and take the sidewalk that wound around the tree. It took less than a minute to reach the end of the sidewalk and the edge of the lake.

"Look, Cindy," Greg whispered and pointed at a small fountain situated almost out of sight behind some large, black, plastic trash bags.

Cindy had spotted it, too. "Oh, it looks so lonely out here. The water is barely dribbling out of its spout. It's not very deep."

"I wonder if there's another fountain around here? This water looks awful dirty, and it's an awful small fountain. I envisioned something larger."

"I think this is it," Cindy said, although she didn't know why she said it.

"I think so, too. I feel like it's the right fountain," Greg said. He didn't know why he felt that way either, but somehow he knew they had found the right fountain.

He took the coin from his pocket. No light at all shone from it. He looked over to where his parents sat. They were busy talking and not looking their way. He looked down at Cindy. She smiled back up at him in excitement.

"What if nothing happens?" he asked, and flipped the coin up in the air. He watched as it flipped over and over and slowly tumbled into the pitiful little fountain.

CHAPTER 5

The coin hit the water and a large splash came back and hit him in the face. Surprised, he reacted by flinching backwards, closing his eyes, and covering his face, but the spraying water never stopped. He stepped backwards only to slip and fall onto the wet ground.

"Cindy!" he laughed, "how about that!"

Suddenly, he realized water still sprayed onto him, and for the first time since the coin landed in the fountain, he looked around. He didn't see Cindy and what he saw, shocked him. In fact, it took him a few seconds of staring before he even understood what he was looking at.

He felt a little dizzy and continued to look around to help get his bearings. Somehow, he now found himself in a damp, dark tunnel, just a few feet behind a waterfall. Water sprayed into the tunnel as the huge waterfall hit the large rocks that jutted out from the tunnel's entrance and into the falling water. The walls to the tunnel were about fifteen feet apart where he sat, but narrowed considerably behind him. He looked away from the waterfall to study the tunnel. He thought he could see a speck of light in the distance, but the tunnel looked dark and uninviting.

He looked back at the waterfall and saw a narrow, rock ledge to his left that led out of the tunnel. Plenty of daylight shone through the waterfall. I'd rather go toward the light, he thought, and walked quickly to the ledge. The water in the center of the falls appeared thick and fell with tremendous speed. Here, at the edge, the water still moved downward with nearly the same speed, but it looked only a few inches thick. He thought he could almost see through it.

Greg held his breath and darted through the waterfall. In an instant, he was out, safe, but thoroughly drenched.

"How am I going to explain to Mom and Dad how I got all wet?" he asked himself. Then it hit him.

Where was he? How did he get here? How would he get back? Would he ever see his parents again? Did Cindy come with him, and if so, where was she?

"Cindy!" Greg shouted and looked around. He realized the sound of the waterfall was so loud that no one more than a few feet away would hear him.

No, he thought, Cindy hadn't come with him. This was his journey, his task. The coin had his name on it, and although he couldn't explain it, this adventure was meant for him alone. Tears welled up in his eyes. He felt so alone. His hand went instinctively to his pocket, but the coin wasn't there.

The waterfall fed a powerful river that raced through the canyon below him. He stood on the side of a very steep hill, or maybe it was a mountain. He couldn't see how high it went. Low thick clouds blocked his vision. Below him the side of the hill consisted mostly of sheer rock. No way he could safely go down. Above him the terrain looked rough and jungle-like with patches of thick green vegetation, but it didn't appear as steep. Better to go up, he thought. He would have to climb, and he began looking for a starting place. He needed something he could grab or a place to get a good foothold. He had only taken a couple of steps when he saw something colorful and moving fast. It seemed to be coming, or falling, straight at him.

Greg's instincts took over, and while his feet wanted him to flee, he stood still and braced himself. The thing came crashing through the bushes directly above him and collided into him. In the process, he fell backwards and nearly over the cliff to certain death below.

"You saved my life!"

Only then did Greg realize what had fallen onto him. It was a she - only more than that. Greg stared into the eyes of a beautiful girl. Her face almost touched his, and her body sprawled on top of him.

"Er, I mean, umh, are you okay?" Greg asked, embarrassed that he was almost stammering.

"Yes, thank you. You saved my life," the girl repeated. She pushed herself up and off him and began to brush the leaves and dirt off herself.

Greg stood up, but kept his eyes on her. She wore clothes like some character in a movie. She had on a bright red dress, only it wasn't like any dress he had seen before. It appeared to be made from one piece of material, maybe leather, he thought, and covered her from her shoulders to her knees. She wore a wide blue belt around her waist. Her arms were exposed from the shoulder, and each wrist was adorned with a wide, jewel encrusted, gold bracelet.

"Quick, they are chasing after me. We must hide!" she said in an urgent, but hushed voice.

She looked up toward the area on the side of the hill from which she had fallen. Greg did the same, not sure what or who she was talking about. Far up the hillside, they both saw movement.

"Quick, before they see me, but where can we go?"

Greg instantly knew where he had to take her.

"Come with me," he said and took a few steps to the edge of the waterfall.

She looked at him as though he was crazy.

"The waterfall will kill us. It will knock us down and carry us to the rocks below."

"There's a way," he said. "Trust me. I just came from in there."

She hesitated for only a few seconds. "I might as well die from the power of the almighty Yung, than perish at the hands of the evil Denza," she said and ran toward him.

Greg extended his hand, and she grabbed it. Then he half pulled her through the edge of the waterfall to the safety of the tunnel behind it.

"You must be a magician to know of this place," she said. Her eyes studied him. "What funny clothes you wear."

"To be honest, I was thinking the same about your clothes. Why are those men chasing you?"

"They are the Denza, they do not want me to get back to my tribe. They are evil," she said.

"You should call the police," Greg suggested.

"The police? What are these police, and how should I call them?"

Suddenly, Greg saw movement through the translucent edges of the waterfall.

"They are out there. I think we should leave," he said, and motioned his head in the direction away from the waterfall. He knew they could not see through the curtain of water into the relative darkness of the tunnel, but he didn't feel safe staying where they were.

"I do not think they will come in here," she replied, "but it would be wiser to move as far away from them as we can."

They started walking deeper into the tunnel.

"Would those men really kill you?" Greg asked.

"Yes. They chase me because I have the proclamation from our King. It proves that the land from the River Yung to the Agate Mountain belongs to my people. It is the proclamation the Denza want to destroy. My death would simply be a minor pleasure for them."

"King? Agate Mountain? The Denza? I don't understand. Minutes ago I was in Florida at Disney World. Certainly you know Disney World." Greg didn't believe there was a child in the entire world who hadn't heard of Disney World.

"I do not know of this Florida, but I do know you are not there. You are in the Valley of the Yung, in the Kingdom of Dragon King. I know there are other lands past ours, but no one dares go there." She looked at him strangely, as though for the first time she was really studying him.

"I don't understand. I don't know where I am or how I got here. I don't even know your name."

"My name is Fawn. I am the second Princess of the Cheerakoo. You shall be rewarded for my rescue."

Cheerakoo? Greg thought it almost sounded like a cereal.

"But what country are we in?" Greg persisted.

"Why do you ask me silly questions? I already told you. This is the Kingdom of the Dragon King. What is your name?"

"Greg."

"Greg," she repeated the name slowly to herself. "I've never heard that name before. It must be an important name if no one else can use it."

"I'm sure someone else around here is named Greg, or maybe Gregory," he said hesitantly.

"No, only you," Fawn said. "Gregory," she said the name slowly to herself. "I like this name Gregory better. It is your name, too?"

"Yes, but ---"

"I shall call you Gregory," Fawn interrupted him.

Greg groaned to himself. Lost in a strange land, being chased by the murderous Denza, clothes soaking wet from the waterfall, and now being called Gregory by this strange girl, what else could go wrong? No sooner had those thoughts cleared his mind, when Greg took a step in the darkness and found himself falling five feet to the ground below.

"Ouch!" Greg shouted as he landed on the hard dirt.

"Why did you step into that hole?" Fawn asked.

"I didn't see it."

"It was in plain sight," she said.

"It's dark in here."

"I know, but you can still see it. You did not step in the last hole."

"I didn't see the last one either," Greg replied.

"That is because you do not have the eyes of the Cheerakoo. Stay close to me. I will point out the holes in the path."

Greg climbed out of the hole. Barely enough light existed to see where Fawn stood.

"It is not far now," Fawn stated.

CHAPTER 6

Greg thought that they hadn't made much progress toward the spot of light that marked the end of the tunnel. But if Fawn said they were making progress, it was good enough for him.

"Why do the Denza want to prevent you from taking the proclamation to your people?"

"They want the Agate Mountain for themselves."

"Can't you share?" Greg asked.

"The Denza do not share. We have tried."

"Why doesn't the King simply tell them to stay off your mountain?"

"It does not work that way. The King does not leave his part of the Kingdom, and he does not enforce the laws. Surely you know this?"

"No, I don't. I'm not from your land, remember? So even with this proclamation of yours, if the King won't enforce the laws, what's to keep the Denza from fighting your people for the mountain?"

"Why the Zeon, of course," Fawn said.

"And who are the Zeon?" Greg wondered if he was experiencing a bad dream. This was getting complicated.

"The Zeon live among us throughout the Kingdom. They are normally a very peaceful race; however, they become a ruthless, invincible force in the defense of a tribe's borders."

"They don't sound so peaceful to me."

"You do not understand. They live among all of us - the

Denza, as well as the Cheerakoo. The Zeon are our friends, they are friends with the Denza, and they are friends with all the other tribes. They live among all of us and would defend the Denza's land, as well as ours, if it were invaded."

"Are they soldiers?"

"No, we have no need for soldiers here in the Kingdom."

"Soldiers or not, I think you should have brought some of your Zeon friends with you on this journey of yours."

"They would not come," Fawn said. Greg noticed she said this in a matter-of-fact voice. She appeared to hold no bitterness with them for not coming.

Greg realized the tunnel had become brighter. They had nearly arrived at the other end. He looked at Fawn and thought that she had to be one of the most beautiful girls he had ever seen. She had light brown skin and long, wavy, almost curly, dark hair. Greg thought Fawn's hair was a very dark brown rather than black. Her eyes were a beautiful, bright green. Now that he thought about it, Greg wondered if Fawn was wearing contact lenses. Her eyes seemed a little brighter than other people's eyes.

"Wow!" Greg exclaimed. "Look at this view."

They reached the end of the tunnel and from the rock ledge he could see for miles over a vast, beautiful jungle valley that lay before him. In the distance, a huge mountain rose high into the sky.

"That is Agate Mountain. The Cheerakoo land covers the entire valley at the base of the mountain. The Denza live up on the plateau and on part of lands that are past the valley."

"Whose land are we now in?" Greg asked.

"This land belongs to everyone."

"I don't see how we can get down from here. We may have to go back."

"It would not be wise to go back. The Denza will believe I am hiding back there. They will leave some of their men there for days to search for me," Fawn said.

"Won't they think that you must have fallen to your death?"

"Yes. They will think that, but they will still search."

Greg looked again at the almost vertical slope below him, and then turned his head to look up.

"I think we can climb up, but it won't be easy," he said.

Fawn studied the side of the hill. Suddenly, she stepped out onto a narrow ledge and started to climb.

"Be careful, and wait for me," Greg said before scurrying out to follow her up.

The climb frightened Greg. More than once his footing slipped, and he thought he was going to fall to a certain death. He kept going, mostly because he wasn't going to let Fawn show him up. Despite his best efforts, he had to admit that she handily beat him to the top.

When he finally crawled over the top of the cliff, he saw her sitting under a thick bush that hid her from anyone looking from any other direction. She motioned for him to be quiet and to come to her. He crawled into the small opening, and the rough leaves on the large bush forced him to sit with his side touching hers. Greg couldn't remember ever seeing a bush like this one.

"We have to be quiet," Fawn whispered to him.

"The Denza?"

"Possibly the Denza, but more so because of him," Fawn replied and pointed.

Greg looked where she pointed and almost jumped up. Fawn grabbed his arm.

"Stay still. He's sleeping."

Greg stared at what she had pointed to. Slightly above them on a rock ledge, a huge saber-toothed tiger slept.

"That can't be," he whispered.

"What do you mean?"

"They're extinct."

"Do you see him?"

"Yes," Greg admitted.

"Do you want to go up there and touch him?"

"No way."

"Then trust me, he is not extinct. They are rare, but they certainly exist. Gregory, you must be from a far-away land. You do not appear to know very much."

Greg was about to agree, when the saber-toothed tiger rose up, sniffed the air, and let out a tremendous roar. He sniffed again, and Greg imagined the tiger sensed their presence. He wanted to ask Fawn what they should do, but he noticed she remained motionless and quiet, so he did the same.

The big cat leapt from the ledge to a spot on the ground a little to their left and just out of sight. Greg looked over to where he thought it was, but the foliage on the bush and the other plants around him made it impossible to see anything. He hoped it was the same for the tiger, in case it was looking in their direction.

Greg worried that at any moment the saber-toothed tiger would appear directly in front of them. If he did there would be no escape for them, no place to hide.

Luckily, a few seconds later, they heard another loud roar

further behind them. The big cat had moved away from them in search of his meal elsewhere. Greg looked over at Fawn, and she looked back at him and smiled.

"That was a close one," she said. "For a moment I thought we might be his supper."

"Me, too."

"Gregory, I think we should move away from this spot. We may be close to his home, and he may return soon."

"Let's go," Greg agreed, "but let's not go in the same direction he went."

"This way," Fawn said. She led him along a narrow path that ran next to the edge of a cliff.

Greg studied the terrain around them. Somehow, the coin must have transported him to Africa. After all, they were in the Animal Kingdom when he threw the coin in the fountain, and he was definitely in a jungle. The clouds had all gone away, and the sun appeared to be larger here than it looked to him when he was home. Maybe this was how the sun looked from Africa.

"Yuck!" Fawn complained as she peeled a giant spider web out of her hair.

"Let me get that," Greg said and pulled the remaining strands off Fawn.

"I hate spiders," she said.

"Well, at least the girls here are the same." He didn't know any girls back home that liked spiders. At least as not as much as he liked them. He thought they were fascinating.

"I do not know what you mean by "the girls here", but thank you for helping me get that nasty web out of my hair."

When they started walking again, with Fawn still in the lead,

Greg glanced to his right and saw a huge spider. At first, he thought it was a giant tarantula, but then he thought something made this spider a little different from the spiders he had seen before. Fawn disappeared around a bend in the trail, so Greg stopped his study of the spider and ran to catch up with her.

"Gregory, where is your land?"

"America," he said.

"I have never heard of this America. I have been wondering. Do they not have the Zeon there?"

"No."

"Hmmm."

In the distance, Greg heard the sound of what he thought was a horn being blown. It paused, and then he heard it again.

"We must hurry. That is the Denza. They may have spotted us."

They both started jogging down the trail.

"I don't see anything," Greg said. "How do you know it's them, or that they see us?"

"They use horns to rally their hunters. They have spotters high up in the trees. Maybe they hunt something else, but maybe not."

They had only run for a couple of minutes when they had to stop suddenly. The path ended at the top of a steep ravine.

"We will have to jump to the other side," Fawn said.

"That looks too far," Greg answered.

"We may not make it, but if we stay here we will surely die at the hands of the Denza."

"Wait a minute, Fawn. If we use that log over there, we may be able to push it across the gap to the other side and use it as a bridge."

They both ran to the log and started dragging it toward the end of the path. Greg estimated that the distance to the other side was about fifteen feet. He hoped the log was long enough. It certainly was heavy. When they reached the edge of the cliff, they started sliding the log out. They had only gotten it about half way when the end over the open ravine started to tilt downward.

"Stop!" Greg shouted. "This won't work. It will fall down if we go much further. Pull it back. I've another idea."

"I think we should try to jump across," Fawn said. For the first time since he'd first caught her, Greg saw that Fawn was becoming noticeably frightened.

"Just give me one more minute," Greg insisted.

He braced the heavier end of the log against the top of a large rock that barely broke the surface of the path and started to lift the other end. Fawn needed no encouragement to come by his side and start lifting, and then pushing the lighter end of the log straight up toward the sky. Together they strained against the weight of the log until it was nearly vertical.

Suddenly, the log's momentum and gravity took over, and the log fell toward the other side of the gorge. It hit with a "kar-wumph," but remained still after hitting the ground and taking a small bounce.

"Quick," Fawn said and sprinted across the log.

The log didn't even shudder under her weight. She was slightly taller than him, but Greg was certain he outweighed her. However, since the log handled her weight so well, he decided to put caution aside and ran across.

"Gregory, let's go," urged Fawn, when Greg hesitated after crossing their homemade bridge.

"No. We have to first get rid of the log." He bent over and strained to pick up the end of the log. This should be the lighter end, he thought, but for whatever reason it took all of his strength to lift it a few inches. Fawn appeared next to him, and in a few seconds, they managed to push their end off the edge. They watched briefly as the log fell, end over end, to the rocks below.

Fawn turned to head back into the jungle when the ground under her back foot gave way beneath her. She instinctively reached out to Greg, who at the same time reached for her. Their hands clasped, and he pulled her onto firmer ground.

"You saved me again, Gregory," she said smiling and squeezed his hand.

CHAPTER 7

Together they moved quickly to the cover of the nearby jungle. Just as they crossed into the dense foliage, an arrow slammed into a tree inches from Greg's head. Soon they were a dozen yards into the jungle and could breathe a sigh of relief.

"Fawn," Greg called for her in a hushed voice. The underbrush had become so thick he could barely see more than a couple feet in any direction.

"Here," Fawn replied.

Greg looked towards the voice. He only saw her as she waved her hand and bright bracelet. He moved in close to her.

"We mustn't get separated, or we'll never find each other in this thick stuff."

In response, she grabbed his hand and pulled him in the direction she wanted to go. As Greg had no idea which way they should go, he moved up beside her and followed her lead while she directed them away from the gorge and the Denza.

After a few hundred yards of very thick jungle, they reached a part of the jungle where thick patches of underbrush were interspersed with fairly open areas.

"If we stick to the open ground and work our way around the thick areas, we will make better time and not get so tired," Fawn said.

"That's good by me," Greg responded, "I'm a bit worn out already. Do you think they found a way across?"

"I do not know. I think it is a long way around, and I did

not see any other logs that they could use like we did, if they even thought to do so. That was a very clever idea, Gregory. But here, let us take a look."

Fawn ran over to a nearby tree and started to climb. She was up the tree as quickly as a squirrel could have shot up one back home, Greg thought. She didn't stop climbing until she was near the top. The heavy underbrush rose for about twenty feet, and the top of the tree towered over it by another twenty.

"What do you see?"

"A small group of them are on the other side, might be eight or nine men. One of them is pointing in this direction."

Greg heard a distant scream.

"One man tried to jump across," she said.

"Sounded like he didn't make it," Greg said.

Fawn climbed down, grabbed his hand, and started running.

"Did they make it across?"

"I do not think so. I think we are safe now, for a while, but I do not know if someone jumped before the one I saw. Still, I think it would be better if we ran for a while."

They ran in silence for about twenty minutes before they hit another solid wall of thick jungle. Greg had seen three different small herds of deer-like creatures in the fields that they passed through. Only one herd sprinted away in fear when he and Fawn ran by. The others seemed cautious but held their ground. The animals intrigued him. Although similar to animals he had seen in zoos, these looked different. Greg was beginning to wonder if he was still on earth.

Fawn grabbed his hand as soon as they entered the thick underbrush. Together they struggled onward. At every turn, the leaves and branches seemed to grab them and try to stop them from going any further. On a few occasions the branches or leaves had thorns on them. Finally, they broke through into a small clearing.

"It will be getting dark soon," Fawn said. "We need to prepare a camp."

"Is it safe here?"

"Here is safe. The Denza cannot find us here."

"I mean from the saber-toothed tiger and other animals," Greg said.

"We are as safe here as anywhere from them, night or day. If they find us they may or may not eat us, but that is nature's way. When it gets dark we will build a fire. That will help keep them away."

Greg started gathering small sticks and a fewer larger ones for the fire. He glanced at Fawn and saw that she had a small knife in her hand and was cutting away at some of the thick bushes.

"That will be too green to burn," he said.

"I am clearing out a hollow for us to sleep in. It will be safer for us than sleeping out in the open. The large birds of the night would see us out there."

"Large birds?" Greg asked.

"Yes, the ornas. They hunt at night. They can be very dangerous."

Greg stacked the sticks together in the manner he learned from his father and then later from the Boy Scouts. He looked up at the sky and wondered what the ornas looked like. All he could see were normal looking birds that didn't appear threatening at all.

Thoughts of his father made him think, for the first time

since arriving in this strange land, of his parents and the worrying they must be going through. He knew Cindy would tell them that he just disappeared when he threw the coin into the fountain, but no one would believe her story. He couldn't blame them, he still wondered if he was having a dream. He pinched himself to try to wake up but nothing happened. If he was in a dream it was the most real one he had ever experienced. He could smell the wild flowers that permeated the jungle. He could hear its sounds, and Fawn sure appeared real enough.

"Here," Fawn said holding out her hand. "You must be hungry, Gregory. Eat these. They are very good."

Fawn's comments caused Greg to realize just how hungry he was. He had eaten a huge breakfast, but nothing since. He reached out his hand and Fawn poured a number of berries that looked like raspberries into it. He stared at them for a second.

"Go on and eat them. They will not poison you."

"I know," Greg responded. He tossed the entire bunch into his mouth. They were absolutely delicious. They tasted much sweeter than any raspberries he had eaten before.

"There are a lot more on that branch," she pointed to a bush exposed by the open hollow that she had cut into the thick underbrush. "There are also some pears on that small tree," she pointed at the other side of the hollow.

Greg crawled into the small enclosure and located a pear. Within minutes it joined the raspberries in his stomach.

"Here," she said again, "drink this." She had cut what appeared to be a cucumber or a zucchini in half. She gave him one half and kept the other for herself.

He looked inside the half she gave him and discovered a

clear liquid filled it nearly to the top. He looked at Fawn and saw her drinking. He took a sip. It tasted just like water, so he drank it all. When he finished, he looked at Fawn and realized she was studying him.

"What is it?" he asked.

"You are not from here, are you?"

"I tried to tell you that," he replied.

"No, I mean you are not from this world."

"I don't know. I come from Earth."

"I do not know this word earth," Fawn said.

"I keep thinking I'm in Africa, but if I could be in Florida in one second and Africa the next, then I guess I could be anywhere."

"We have stories about faraway lands and even stories about people who come from the stars to help our people or to harm them."

"I don't know how I got here, Fawn, but I'm not here to harm you or anyone."

"I know that, Gregory. You are here to help me. That is what you are doing, no?"

"Yes, it seems so. For some reason, I feel that it is what I must do."

Fawn smiled and squeezed his hand. "It will soon be dark. We should light the fire."

Greg almost said that he didn't have any matches, but Fawn slid past him and moved toward the small pile of sticks. She reached into a hidden pocket in her dress and pulled out a small amount of white powder. She sprinkled it over the wood and brushed her hands together to ensure all the powder had fallen over the sticks. She then plucked a red jewel off the bracelet on her left wrist and struck it against the same bracelet. A large spark jumped from the bracelet to the wood and a fire immediately erupted.

"Fascinating," Greg said.

"You picked good wood for the fire. It will last a long time. Let us go back inside and finish our hideaway."

Greg followed her, not sure what else they needed to do.

In the small space, Fawn quickly went to work gathering up all the branches she had cut to make the hollow. She used these to build a thin front wall to their enclosure. By the time she had finished, Greg had to admit he could barely see the fire even though it was only a few feet away.

"We should be safe now," she said. Without saying another word she curled up on the ground and closed her eyes.

Greg felt a little uncomfortable. He had never been on a campout with a girl, and other than his sister he had never slept this close to a girl. He didn't even know if he could lie down without touching her.

He pressed himself against the bushes opposite her and stretched out. The soft grass gave off a mild, lemon scent and its soft thickness gave him the illusion he was on a bed. Despite his concerns, in a few seconds he fell fast asleep.

A noise outside the enclosure startled him. He sat up and nearly bumped into Fawn who knelt by the entrance, her knife in hand. He knew better than to make a sound. Could the saber toothed tiger have found them?

No light came from where the fire had been, but he imagined a bright moon shone from the sky as twilight seemed to permeate the surroundings. He could barely make out the large, shadowy figure that moved around outside.

Suddenly, a second shadow descended nearby, for a moment blocking the light from the moon. It must have landed near the other creature, because a loud din erupted. One of the creatures did not seem to be very happy about the other's presence. To Greg, it sounded like two giant mockingbirds fighting over their territory.

The loud birdlike noises paused and Greg heard another noise that sounded like the clashing of beaks. The shrieking resumed, and Greg pressed his face closer to the entrance in an attempt to watch the action. Fawn reached over and grabbed his shoulder. He looked at her, and she shook her head at him.

Greg remained still. His new position gave him a slightly better angle to look through the thin front façade. Two prehistoric pterodactyls snapped and snarled at each other only a few yards away from him. One leaped into the air to make his escape, and the other quickly followed it, snapping at it in the air.

Fawn and Greg remained still in the silence until they were sure the creatures were gone.

Fawn put her knife back into her hidden pocket and lay back down as if nothing had happened. Greg's heart raced, and he figured he would not be able to sleep for the rest of the night.

"Where in the world am I?" Greg thought to himself. Maybe he was still on earth, just thousands of years earlier, he thought. That would explain the saber toothed tiger and the pterodactyls.

Fawn's steady breathing indicated that she was already asleep. Brave girl, he thought, and decided that he must try to sleep some more, too.

However, sleep didn't come easy. The thought of his parents franticly searching for him bothered him. He wished he had a way to let them know he was okay. He wondered if he would have to stay forever in this new land. The coin sent him here, he was sure of that, but he no longer had the coin. Without the coin, how could he return?

The more he thought about it, the more certain he became that he had either traveled back in time thousands of years or the coin had sent him to an entirely different world.   Neither seemed possible, yet here he was.

CHAPTER 8

"You are awake?" Fawn asked.

"Yes. After the visit by the large birds last night, I think you called them ornas, I had a hard time going back to sleep."

"That is silly. They did not eat us. They flew away. When they are gone they are harmless. You should have slept. You will be tired today."

Greg smiled at her simple, straightforward logic. "Do we have far to go today?"

"Our journey will not end today, maybe tomorrow. We have to visit the Old Prophet tonight. It is on our way and will be a safe place to stay."

"Okay," Greg responded. He knew he had to depend on Fawn to get him to a place of relative safety. He also believed that his purpose here in this strange world was to help her complete her mission. It was the one thing he'd felt fairly certain of ever since she'd fallen into his arms by the waterfall.

Fawn reached up and pulled a berry off a branch directly above her head.

"Why do we need to visit this prophet?" Greg asked.

"I had a dream last night about you. I saw you floating down from the sky, from the stars. I called out at you and asked you why you had come. You did not say anything, Gregory, you simply pointed to the Old Prophet's house. So, I believe we must go there tonight."

"I don't remember floating down to your world, Fawn, but

as I can't explain how I actually arrived here, I look forward to hearing what the Old Prophet can tell us. What is his name?"

"His name is the Old Prophet. That is all I have ever heard anyone call him."

"But he's a real prophet, right?"

"Of course, he is a prophet."

Greg thought about it for a moment before speaking. "Should we get started? It looks light enough out there."

"Yes, but first let's eat and drink. This place has served us well."

The fruit satisfied Greg's hunger, and it tasted good, but Greg started hoping that at some point he could get his hands on a hamburger.

"Do you think the ornas are still gone?" Greg asked while they peeled away the false front to their hideout.

"They hunt at night. During the day they stay in their caves in the mountains. We will be safe from them."

The brilliant morning sun proved Fawn right. Other than a few brightly colored butterflies, Greg didn't see any animals in the clearing. The different shades of green in the grasses, bushes and taller trees contrasted sharply with the hundreds of red and yellow flowers that seemed to be everywhere. A beautiful blue sky complemented the scene.

"It's beautiful here," Greg said.

"Only the barren deserts are not beautiful," Fawn said without elaborating further. "We must travel toward the rising sun now. When we reach the Blue River, we will be near the Old Prophet's land."

"You lead, and I'll follow."

"It does not matter who leads," she said.   "It is only

important that we do not get separated."

It took only a few minutes to cross the clearing, and soon they found themselves again traveling through a thick, unyielding jungle. The sweet fragrance of the flowers and various fruits almost overwhelmed Greg. On two occasions he had to sneeze, and finally, he cupped his hands over his mouth and nose while they traveled through the worst of the areas. He didn't have any allergies that he knew of, but then this wasn't his earth.

"You do not like the smell of our flowers?" Fawn asked when they finally broke through to open terrain.

"Actually, they smell delicious. There were just too many of them."

"Wait for one minute," Fawn said. She went back to the edge of the thick underbrush and plucked a small, bright red flower from a thick vine. She returned to him and held her hand with the flower out to him. "Here, eat this."

"Eat the flower?"

"Yes. When our babies show a discomfort around these flowers we feed them the flower. It heals them."

"Seriously?" Greg asked.

"What?"

"Never mind," he said. Of course, she was serious. He hadn't seen her be anything but serious since he met her. He took the flower from her and popped it into his mouth. Surprisingly, despite its bright color and strong sweet fragrance, the flower had no taste at all. He chewed it up and swallowed it.

Fawn had already started walking, so Greg trotted to catch up with her.

"Good idea, Gregory" she said. "We should run. Staying too long out in the open like this will expose us the Denza. The forest ahead will provide more safety."

Greg didn't tell her that the need to run hadn't really been an idea of his. However, if she wanted to think he had a good idea, then that was good enough for him. As it was, he had trouble enough keeping up with her. She ran at a steady pace that he could barely match, and he didn't know how long he could stay with her. He positioned himself two steps behind her and just off to her side.

He watched her run. She impressed him with the ease with which she seemed to carry herself. She had long smooth strides. He noticed that while he was soon breathing hard and sweating, she appeared to be as calm and refreshed as when they started running. No wonder her parents named her Fawn, she could run like a deer.

Although Fawn had referred to a forest being ahead of them, they had run for a good fifteen minutes before Greg could see any signs of a forest in the distance. Meanwhile, small clumps of trees provided a patchwork of plant life in the grassy, rolling plains. Once again, Greg saw small herds of grazing deer-like animals in the distance. They showed no interest in the two jogging across their land.

"We'll need to walk the rest of the way," Fawn announced as they came to the top of a small rise.

Greg gladly stopped running. For the past several minutes, he had resisted his growing need to ask her if they could walk for a while. Thoroughly exhausted, he gazed out at the extreme change in terrain that covered the last five hundred yards before the edge of the forest.

"During the floods, this land is taken over by the Yung. The great river's waters move so swiftly it brings down the large rocks from the mountains. While it is now dry, we cannot run through it."

Hearing her explanation, Greg could see that the terrain between them and the forest did resemble a wide, fairly shallow, dry river bed. Thousands, perhaps millions, of rocks ranging from small river pebbles to boulders as large as small cars were scattered throughout the river bed in both directions as far as his eyes could see.

"Fascinating," Greg said. "How often do the floods occur?"

"Every year, around the third full moon. The floods are usually gone by the fourth moon. Do not worry we have two more moons before the next floods come."

They started walking into the river bed.

"Do you have months here, Fawn?"

"You mean the period between full moons? Of course we do."

"I mean like June, July and August. Do you name your months?"

"No. We just number the moons."

"How many months, or moons, do you have in a year?" Greg asked.

She looked at him strangely. "Ten, of course," she paused for a second, "what about where you come from Gregory? How many moons do you have?"

"In my world," he said, for the first time really believing he must be on a different planet entirely, "we have twelve months in a year."

The stone covered river bed made for rough walking. After

they traveled about a third of the way across, Greg stopped and looked back in the direction they had come. The larger boulders blocked his view. He moved closer to Fawn. A guy could get lost in here, he thought.

Smack! In an instant, Greg's serene new world took a frightening twist. A very large snake struck at Fawn. Somehow, she had ducked just in time and the huge serpent struck the side of a giant boulder. The snake appeared larger than even the giant anacondas he'd seen once on television.

The snake semi-coiled itself before it struck again at Fawn. She reacted by leaping to her left and slid into a narrow spot between two large rocks. The snake squeezed its head into the small space in an effort to grab Fawn with its teeth, but Fawn stabbed it with her knife. The snake drew its head back out and attempted to push the smaller of the two stones away from the larger one.

Greg didn't think the snake, as big as it was, would be able to budge the rocks, but sure enough, one of the rocks moved an inch or two.

"Run! Gregory, save yourself, run!" Fawn hollered at him.

His first instinct was to turn and flee, and he did run for about ten yards before he stopped himself. He couldn't abandon Fawn. The coin didn't bring him here to this mysterious place just to run away. He turned and looked back at Fawn and the snake. Any moment now and the snake would have the smaller of the two large boulders moved far enough to fully expose Fawn.

Greg grabbed a softball sized stone from a cluster of similar rocks at his feet. He threw it at the snake and hit it squarely a few feet below its head. The snake twisted and shook its head, but did not seem to realize what had happened.

"I wonder if it even knows I'm here," he said softly to himself. He hurled another rock at the same spot on the snake. As before, the rock solidly hit the snake, and the snake began to writhe in pain. This time, however, the snake moved away from Fawn and looked around to find its attacker.

Greg ducked behind a large rock, terrified that at any second the giant snake would be upon him. After a few seconds, when nothing had happened, he peeked out around the corner of the boulder to find the snake. It had gone back to its attack on Fawn. The snake had already forced its head deeper into the small gap where Fawn hid.

Greg saw Fawn's arm going up and down as she tried to defend herself with her knife. The snake would partially draw its head out and then resume its attack. Greg didn't know how much longer Fawn could stave off the crushing bite of the large snake.

He spotted a basketball sized rock near the snake. He raced to the rock, lifted it above his head with all his strength, and threw it down as hard as he could on the back of the snake. He heard a crunching sound as the rock struck the body of the snake. The width of the snake's body exceeded that of the rock that had smashed against it, but only by a few inches.

In a blink of an eye, the large snake's head darted out of the small gap and straight at Greg. Greg instinctively jumped away from the snake's attack, and the side of the snake's head knocked him further away as it shot by. The jaws of the great snake snapped shut as the head made contact with him, but other than ripping his shirt the sharp teeth did no damage.

Rather than follow up with another attack on Greg or Fawn

the snake repeatedly coiled and uncoiled itself as it writhed in pain. From the way it moved, Greg thought that he may have broken the snake's back.

Suddenly, a hand grabbed his arm.

"Hurry, Gregory, we must go!"

He needed no further encouragement, and they both ran as best they could through the remainder of the river bed to the forest on the other side. They didn't stop running until they were well hidden among the trees.

CHAPTER 9

"**A**re you okay, Fawn?"

"Yes. Why did you not run away and save yourself? That would have been the wise thing to do."

"I couldn't leave you alone with that snake!"

"You are very brave, Gregory, and the best stone thrower I have ever seen."

"I play baseball."

"I don't know what this baseball is, but you have saved my life again. I am not sure how I can ever repay you. I will be in your debt forever."

"I just did what anyone would do."

"No, I do not believe there are many who would have done what you have done for me today. To stand and fight the giant serpent is something few have ever lived to tell about it. We are taught that it is better for one to die, than for two to die."

"It is best for no one to die," Greg stated.

Fawn smiled at him, "Perhaps so."

They continued to walk among the tall trees, staying close to the forest edge as it paralleled the dry river bed.

"We should get to the prophet's land soon. Then we will safe from the Denza," Fawn informed him.

"Do you think they are still pursuing you?"

"Yes. They are back there somewhere. You can be sure of that."

"I'm kind of dirty to meet someone. I guess there's not a

place where I can wash my clothes, or a place a guy could take a shower before we get there?"

"You are fine. While we are at his home, I am sure we will get a chance to clean up."

"Have you met him before?" Greg asked.

"Of course. He has even been a guest at my parents' home. I was younger then, but he will remember me."

"I'll certainly always remember you," Greg said quietly to himself.

"What?"

"Oh, nothing, I was just thinking out loud."

"You are a strange young man, Gregory."

"I don't know. I think I'm fairly normal."

"You are very brave, but you still speak like a young one."

"What do you mean?"

"You combine your words. We learn as we get older not to do that."

"You mean contractions?"

"Yes, Gregory, what else would I mean?"

Greg didn't say anything, but he realized that was why she sounded so formal when she talked. She hadn't been using any contractions.

"It is all right. You may speak like a young one, but I know you are very brave and smart."

Greg beamed but remained silent.

Suddenly, they found themselves at a corner of the forest. To their left, the large dry river bed still bordered the forest. Straight ahead, a slow moving river, barely thirty yards across, blocked their passage. Greg thought that the river appeared to be low, which he imagined made sense since the other river bed was completely dry. This small river merged with the larger dry river bed and gently curved away from them, filling a small section of the larger river bed as it meandered out of sight.

"The Blue River. Its water is low. Maybe the rains will come sooner this year."

Fawn started walking away from the dry river bed, and Greg quickly joined her. They followed the river, and Fawn stayed out in the open rather than in the trees as they had before.

"Shouldn't we be inside the tree line? We can be easily seen out here."

"I think we are safe for now. We are on, or very near, the prophet's land. The Denza will not attack us in here."

"I still don't understand what prevents the Denza from attacking us, no matter where we are."

"The Zeon do not tolerate the Denza's aggressive behavior in land that belongs to someone else. It is the way it has always been."

"Can't the Denza defeat the Zeons?"

"No one can defeat the Zeons."

"Then what's to stop the Zeons from taking everyone's land for their own?"

"Nothing, but they have never done so. It is something we have asked ourselves, too. We do not really know why the Zeons behave as they do. Our history has stories of entire civilizations destroying themselves through civil wars, and the Zeons have done nothing. Yet if one Denza, or if even I, were to try to seize one small piece of someone else's land the Zeon would respond ferociously."

"Haven't the Zeon given you an explanation for their

behavior?"

"Ha! They might if they could. We have never been able to communicate, in the real sense, with them."

"What do you mean?"

"You try it," Fawn said and nodded her head toward the forest.

Greg looked to his right, and barely ten feet inside the edge of the forest, he saw two apelike creatures, thin but about seven feet tall, walking toward them. He gasped.

"They will not harm us," Fawn said, sensing his fear.

Greg realized that the two Zeon carried fishing poles. A reddish brown fur covered the Zeon from head to toe. They looked intensely at Greg as they passed him on their way to the river.

"I don't think they like me," he said.

"They probably sense something different about you. They are very intelligent."

"They didn't have any nets. What will they do with any fish they catch?"

"They will eat them immediately," Fawn explained. "They are very good hunters and fishers. There are some more Zeon over there." She pointed to a clearing in the forest that extended nearly a quarter of a mile from the river.

"There are a lot of them," Greg said, some of his fear returning.

"I wonder," Fawn said half to herself.

"Wonder what?"

"Oh, nothing. Look up there, Gregory. On that small hill, that dwelling belongs to the Old Prophet."

"I see it. Wow, it looks cool!"

"I am sure he keeps it as cool as he can, but how can you tell that from here?"

"It's an expression we use where I come from. I meant to say I like the way it looks," Greg explained.

For the moment, Greg forgot about the Zeon and the Denza. As they approached the prophet's home, he marveled at its appearance. It didn't look like any house he'd ever seen before. The house, or dwelling as Fawn referred to it, was larger than his own home, but the house only served as the centerpiece of a more amazing design. Beautifully manicured bushes and flowers of every imaginable color covered most of the yard. Several large trees with wide green canopies appeared to stand guard around the house. Next to the house, a gazebo stood as the only visible out structure. Vines full of red and white flowers wrapped themselves around the wooden beams that supported the gazebo's roof.

The house sparkled where the sun successfully penetrated the trees and reflected against it. When they got closer, Greg discovered that hundreds of large jewels had been pressed into the grout that held together the rock front to the house. Greg guessed the jewels were rubies, emeralds, and other precious stones.

"I'm surprised that those jewels haven't been stolen," Greg said when they stopped immediately in front what appeared to be the edge of the front yard.

"It would not be wise to make the prophet mad."

"But they're valuable here in your land, aren't they?"

"Of course. Many people would trade a lot of food or other goods for a nice gemstone."

"The prophet must be very wealthy."

"I guess he may be," said Fawn, "but the gemstones are more of a symbol of status."

Greg looked again at Fawn's two jewel encrusted bracelets. She did say she was a princess, so perhaps the bracelets reflected her rank.

It dawned on Greg that this was the first house he had seen since his arrival in this strange land.

"Does your house look like this one?" he asked.

"Our home is entirely different. It is much, much larger, but many people live in it, too. You will see."

"I hope to."

"Ahh! Princess Fawn, I have been awaiting your arrival."

Greg looked over at the Gazebo, to where the voice had come, and saw a very old man with long stringy white hair and beard. He supported himself with crutches and smiled broadly when Fawn acknowledged his presence.

"Oh, it is so good to see you again, my grand sir!" Fawn said as she moved toward the old man.

To his surprise, the prophet did a partial bow as Fawn approached him.

"No, please, it is my honor to be here," Fawn said.

The two hugged each other, and as they separated, the prophet turned his attention toward Greg.

"So, you are him," the old man stated. "We should all go inside for refreshments."

Greg wondered what he meant when he said "you are him," but decided to ask him later. At hearing the word refreshments, Greg realized how famished he was. The three went into the house.

They were met just inside the house by a short woman

carrying a tray with three wooden bowls containing a light bluish liquid. Greg wondered how she knew they would be arriving.

"Please," she said, offering the drinks to them.

After Fawn and the prophet took theirs, Greg accepted the final bowl. He saw that Fawn drank the liquid straight from the bowl. He did the same and was amazed how much the beverage tasted like lemonade.

"Thank you, this is very delicious," he said.

"Of course it is," Fawn said in a tone that Greg thought was admonishing him.

He looked at the prophet, whose eyes seemed to twinkle in delight.

"That is all right. I have a feast being prepared for us and we have a lot to talk about, but first, I thought you two would like to rest and bathe. Molina," the prophet addressed the small woman who had served the drinks. "Please show them to their rooms."

"This way," Molina said. She guided them around a circular hallway that Greg would have sworn took them in a complete circle. However, rather than end up back where they started, they stopped by two doors on opposite side of the hall.

"This one is for you, Princess," she said and nodded at the door to their right. "I will come and knock when it is time for dinner. Your bath has been drawn."

"Thank you," Fawn answered and entered her room.

"And you, sir," Molina motioned at the opposite door.

Greg entered, wondering if anyone had ever called him sir before. He turned to thank Molina, but she had already closed the door and departed. He studied the large room he had been assigned. It had no exterior windows, but a large opening in the roof that appeared to be a skylight without the glass allowed in fresh air. One of the large trees shaded the opening from direct sunlight.

Greg thought the flooring was marble. A large, green woven mat covered a portion of the floor. A small wooden table with two chairs sat in one corner of the room. On it Greg saw a bowl of small fruit, none that he readily recognized. In the middle of the far wall was a large round bed covered with furs of all shapes and sizes. A wicker dresser stood next to him on the near wall. The room seemed extremely quiet with the exception of the sound of running water that came from an adjacent room that Greg correctly assumed was the bathroom.

A narrow open archway provided access to the bathroom. Greg peered through it. The running water seemed to be coming from behind a curtain at the end of the bathroom. Greg walked over to it and pulled it open.

Three things immediately struck him as curious. First, he had to use a lot of strength simply to open the curtain. Second, the air in the room behind the curtain was filled with steam, limiting his sight to a few feet. The third curious thing was that he sensed the bath, if that was what it really was, extended for quite a distance.

He loosened his grip on the curtain, and it snapped back into place against the wall. He walked over to the sink. It took him a few moments studying the sink to figure out how it worked. By pumping a small handle located on the side of a pipe next to the sink, water would flow out of lion's mouth shaped spigot and into a bowl that appeared to be a large sea shell. The water was ice cold.

He considered using the small cloth next to the sink to wash himself, but he knew the last two days worth of dirt and sweat required more than just some cold water on a small wash cloth. Hesitantly, he removed his clothing and placed them on the bed. He walked back into the bathroom, pulled the curtain open wide enough to step through and stuck a foot into the water. From the amount of steam he thought the water would be quite hot, but actually he found it to be a comfortable temperature.

Greg stepped further into the bath and let the curtain snap shut behind him. He located a small sponge, but no soap, on the side of the bath and started scrubbing himself.

"Interesting," he said to himself. The sponge emitted soapy bubbles as he rubbed it over his body. He didn't like the flowery scent that came with it, but only because he didn't think it was very manly to bathe with a perfumed soap.

The water came barely to his waist, but he noted that the further he got from where he entered the bath the deeper the bath became. In his bathing efforts, he had taken a couple of steps away from the curtain. Curiosity inspired him to take a few more steps away from the curtain. The water moved quickly up to his chest.

He looked back at the curtain and discovered he could no longer see it through the steam. The width of the bath had not increased. The side walls stood about eight feet apart, so Greg decided to keep moving away from the curtain. As long as he stayed in the middle, he could keep sight of the side walls and believed he wouldn't get lost. The size of the bath intrigued him.

The depth did not change any more. He took another ten

strides when a noise startled him. Something was in the water with him. He couldn't help but remember the large snake they had encountered earlier in the day. He stood still and stared hard in attempt to see through the steam.

"Are you spying on me?" Fawn suddenly asked.

"What! Oh no, excuse me, I didn't know you --"

"I forget. Your eyes do not work very well," Fawn interrupted.

This time the voice seemed to come from a different spot.

Greg took a few steps back the way he had come.

"I'm very sorry, Fawn. I didn't know you were in here."

"That is okay. I was just teasing you about spying on me." It sounded as though Fawn had moved again.

"But how did you get into my bath?"

"It is a shared bath."

"Is anyone else in here with us?"

"No. The bath runs from your room to mine. No one else has access to it."

Greg looked around, but he still couldn't see Fawn.

"Well, I'd better get back to my room and get dressed for dinner." Greg moved slowly towards his room. As the water level started to get lower, exposing more of his body, he looked back toward Fawn. He wondered how good her eyes were in seeing through the thick steam. Fighting embarrassment, he hurried the rest of the way to safety on the far side of the curtain. He couldn't be sure, but he thought he heard Fawn giggling as the curtain snapped shut behind him.

CHAPTER 10

When he returned to his bedroom, he noticed that someone had removed his clothes from the bed where he had tossed them, and in their place, left a white bathrobe. He tried on the bathrobe. It felt a little big, but would do. Refreshed and relaxed now, after the bath and despite the slight embarrassment of encountering Fawn in the bath, Greg considered taking a nap.

However, as soon as he got comfortable on the big bed, someone knocked on his door.

"Come in," he said.

The door opened and Molina entered. "Dinner is ready, please come."

"Molina, someone has taken my clothes. I can't go to dinner."

"You have the robe," Molina replied.

"Come on, Gregory," Fawn appeared behind Molina. "I am starved."

Greg noticed that Fawn wore a white bathrobe that looked similar to his.

"Like this? Shouldn't we get dressed?"

"Are your clothes in your room?"

"No."

"Then you should go as you are. I believe they are waiting for us."

Embarrassed for the second time in less than an hour, Greg followed Fawn and Molina down the hallway. The marble flooring felt cold under his bare feet.

When they stepped out of the hallway, Greg expected to be in the large open foyer they had been in before being taken to their rooms. Somehow, though, this time the hallway took them directly to a large dining room. Greg first thought that the room had been converted to a dining room, but on a more thorough study he realized this was an entirely different room.

A large picture window, exposing the beautiful valley below, covered nearly one whole wall. A triangle shaped wooden table sat in the middle of the room.

"Princess, this is your seat," Molina said as she pulled back a heavy, wooden chair for Fawn. "And, this one is yours, Gregory," Molina used his name while she pulled back another one of the chairs for him.

"Thank you." He had barely gotten himself positioned at the table when a tall man in a long robe brought a platter of food to the table. The sight and aroma of a large roast, surrounded by what he supposed were vegetables, reminded him that hadn't had a real meal since breakfast the day before. Focused on the food, he did not see the Old Prophet join them at the table.

"I hope the dinner's appearance is acceptable to you, Gregory."

"Oh, most certainly, sir. It looks delicious."

"Then maybe we should eat first and have our conversation afterwards."

Greg looked over at Fawn. She smiled at him and said, "I am hungry, too."

"This is delicious," Greg remarked as he helped himself to a second helping.

"You have already said that," Fawn said.

"I know, but it's worth repeating."

The prophet smiled broadly at the repeated compliment.

During the meal, the limited conversation pertained to the food and responses to the prophet's questions concerning their satisfaction with the rooms. At the end of the main course, the tall man brought out bowls of small berries covered with a sweet cream. Greg noted self-consciously that he finished his dessert way before his two dinner companions. Once they had finished, the tall man cleared the table and brought each of them a mug of a hot, steaming drink.

"Now we shall have our conversation," the prophet said. His voice sounded almost sinister to Greg. "We are at a very grave time for our world."

"Our world?" Fawn asked.

"Yes, my child. You believe your mission is important for your people, and it is, but it is also critical for the existence of our entire civilization."

"I do not understand."

"I would be surprised if you did. I have studied the prophesies for many years, my Princess, and yet I only grasped the gravity of our situation when I learned of Gregory's arrival."

"My arrival?"

"Yes. You know, you are not the first. Long, long ago, another like you came and helped us. Princess, you may recall the legend of Donovan the Strong."

"Of course, I do," she replied. As she answered, Greg noticed Fawn staring inquisitively at him.

"The Denza's aggressiveness is unique in our world. For many generations, no other tribe has so aggressively tried to expand their territory."

"But the Zeon --"

"I know about the Zeon, my dear," the prophet interrupted Fawn. "So far the Denza's aggression has been carefully orchestrated. They have only taken over lands that were under dispute or unclaimed. You understand this, Princess. That is why you undertook this dangerous mission. If the Denza succeed in preventing you from completing it, they will most certainly move into the land under dispute and even fight to control it. They have already grown more powerful than any other tribe."

Greg noticed that Fawn nodded at their host's remarks.

"Your land is the key. Your people have always been peaceful and tolerant. The Abero tribe that borders you to the north has vast lands that have never been legally registered to it. Your tribe has always honored their borders."

"Of course we have. We have no need for their land, and they have never been concerned with our passage through it or our herds grazing on it."

"The Abero's land and through it the vast uncharted lands that surround us all is the Denza's goal."

"What? That does not make sense. Why would the Denza want all that land? Even a tribe of their size cannot manage all that land."

"They do not care for the land. It only provides them with the means to control the rivers and the prairies. It also gives them access to the three migratory passageways for the Zeon."

"The Zeon migrate?" Greg asked, fully absorbed into the conversation.

"Yes," answered Fawn. "In fact, they are nomadic."

"There are three passageways through which the Zeon enter our realm from the outer world."

"What is the outer world?" Greg asked the prophet.

"It is all of our world that is outside our realm. It is a vast expanse, virtually unexplored. On a few occasions men have traveled into it; if they returned at all they described it as a very dangerous and inhospitable place, unsuitable for our people. We have more than enough land in our realm, and life, for the most part, is pleasant and peaceful."

"The Zeon," Fawn explained, "come and go from our lands through these routes."

"So the Denza want to close off these routes?" Greg asked. "But wouldn't that just make the Zeon mad at them?"

"Probably so. It would be a dangerous thing for the Denza to do, but they would not do it right away. The first step would be to seize the large section of land from your people, Princess, the land now identified in the charter you are carrying, and then go after the Abero's undocumented land. After they accomplished that, they would spend years building their strength before they risked antagonizing the Zeon."

"What would happen if they cut off the migratory routes for the Zeon?" Greg asked.

"No one really knows. Legend has it that the Zeon must return to the outer world every year or they will die, but we do not know if the Zeon will see the blockage of the routes as an act of aggression directed at them or not. Even I do not fully understand why the Zeon behave the way they do."

"We have known for generations that without the Zeon, the Denza would have attacked their neighbors long ago," Fawn added.

"And the king does nothing to prevent this," Greg said, more as a statement than a question.

"For a millennium, the kings have not had to. I do not believe he would know how," the prophet said.

"So you see, Gregory, it is imperative that I get this proclamation to our people," Fawn said.

"But I still don't understand how delivering the proclamation to your people results in the Zeon protecting the disputed lands. I mean how do the Zeon know what's in the King's proclamation?"

Fawn looked to their host to answer Greg's question.

"A very good question that has a very complicated answer. No one really knows, but I have a theory that I believe is near to the truth. The boundaries to all tribal lands are registered and displayed at many public locations throughout the realm. While any tribe can claim whatever land they deem should be theirs, no one can trump the King's proclamations."

"You will see our central registry when we deliver this proclamation," Fawn told Greg.

"More importantly," the prophet spoke again, "these displays are in public parks that are frequented by the Zeon. In fact, the Zeon are seemingly drawn to these parks on their travels. That's always been a curiosity for most people, but I believe they somehow absorb the knowledge from the displays."

"How could they do that?" Greg asked.

The prophet walked over to a nearby table and retrieved a large book. He opened the book and showed a picture to Greg. In the middle of the picture, Greg could easily make out a multi-color map. The map was surrounded by well manicured plants and flowers. Two young children standing together and a Zeon were displayed in the picture studying the map. At the bottom of the picture were the words, "So we learn."

"That picture was drawn over a hundred years ago. Do you notice the different colors in the map?"

"Yes."

"Those colors distinguish lands deeded by the King, other land claimed by a certain tribe, and open lands. Somehow the Zeon absorbs this information and can link it to actual territory. We know birds and other migratory animals are capable of traveling thousands of miles each year without getting lost."

"They follow the stars and the earth's magnetic field," Greg explained, reciting something he had learned from school.

The prophet smiled at him. Greg remembered Fawn saying that she had never heard of the earth. "From my planet, I mean," he added.

"I know what you mean."

The prophet looked at Fawn and then Greg. "Somehow the Zeon can translate the color coded territories on the public maps and understand who rightfully owns what lands. It is in their nature then to protect those lands from outside aggression."

"Fascinating," Greg said.

"This is why you two are in grave danger, but your mission must succeed."

"How do you know of the danger we are in?" Greg asked.

"Can you tell when a storm is coming, Gregory?"

"Yes, usually."

"And, if it is a really bad storm?"

"Most of the time."

"Well for the last few days, I have felt like a very dangerous event was coming closer. Then I learned of your arrival, and my dreams have become focused."

"How did you learn of my arrival?"

"I was told," the prophet answered matter-of-factly. Greg still didn't understand but decided to let it pass.

"As I speak, the Denza have increased their presence around my land. Even the Zeon have sensed it and have become excited. I noticed more Zeon around my home today than I have ever seen before."

"Certainly they would not attack us here," Fawn said.

"I do not believe they will, but they are making it nearly impossible for you to leave."

"What have your dreams told you?" Fawn asked.

"My dreams told me of your impending arrival, Gregory. They also told me that we are at a pivotal point in our world's history. That is why your mission must succeed, Princess."

"Didn't your dreams tell you if she will succeed or not? Will she get the proclamation back to her people?" Greg asked.

"Often it is that simple. This one is more difficult, and your arrival brings its own prophesy. You have arrived from the stars. That has only happened once before. I mentioned him a moment ago, Donovan the Strong."

Fawn turned and stared at Greg, her eyes widening even more.

"Who is this Donovan?" Greg asked.

"It is said that Donovan arrived from the stars just in time to help our first king win the War of Ages. That victory gave birth to our civilization. A way of life that exists to this day, and it ended centuries of warfare and barbaric attacks. That happened many, many generations ago. Fortunately, for the most part, we have lived in peace ever since."

"What happened to Donovan?"

"He died in the final battle," Fawn said.

"Actually, while most people believe just that, it is more correct to say that he disappeared in the final battle. His body was never found, and there is no further mention of him in our history after that final victory."

"So, maybe he didn't die but returned to where he came from," Greg said, thinking of himself. Without the coin, though, how could he return?

"Maybe so," the prophet replied. "At least we can hope so."

"But I'm just a teenager," Greg said. "How can I help you fight the Denza?"

"You are a great warrior, Gregory," Fawn said. "You have already saved my life on three occasions, and you defeated the giant serpent."

Her praise made Greg blush.

"Actually, Gregory, no one wants a war with the Denza. The success of Princess Fawn's mission will avert a war, and I believe your calling is to help her succeed. Hopefully, no one will have to fight the Denza. But I worry....," the prophet let his voice trail off.

"What is wrong?" Fawn asked.

"We must move fast. I sense more Denza arriving. They will bring fire and devastation."

"But certainly the Zeon will not let them!" Fawn exclaimed.

"Right now we are safe," the prophet said calmly, "and you both need to get some sleep. To your rooms and rest easy, I have a plan."

As the three stood up, Fawn grabbed Greg's hand and held

onto it as she led him back to their rooms.

"I am very glad you came to help me, Gregory. I now know that we will succeed."

Greg wanted to ask her how he could make a difference. He didn't think he would be able to fight off the Denza if they ever caught up with them. Deep down, he really just wanted to go home. He fought off these concerns, however, and looked deeply into her lovely eyes. He wondered if there was anyone back on earth this beautiful.

"We'll make it," he said and went into his room before she could see the doubt in his eyes.

"What am I going to do?" Greg said to himself after he closed the door behind him.

CHAPTER 11

He noticed his clothes and a book had been placed on the bed. The clothes looked and even smelled clean. The book had a bookmark in it, so Greg opened to the marked page. He saw a picture of a man, who looked around twenty years old, centered on the page. He immediately noticed the man wore jeans. None of the few people he had seen here wore anything that looked like jeans. He read the caption below the picture, "Donovan the Strong".

Forgetting his own predicament, he climbed into bed and began reading the chapter about Donovan and the Great War. As he did, he saw the similarities to himself. Donovan had arrived suddenly and wore a "strange" style of clothing. Subsequent attempts to trace his past determined that he was not of this world. The book described him as a fierce warrior with an uncanny knowledge of military tactics and strategy. The chapter inferred that he singlehandedly changed the outcome of the Great War.

One sentence really caught Greg's eye. When asked where he learned so much about warfare, Donovan had replied West Point. The author indicated all subsequent efforts failed to figure out where or what West Point was.

The author opined Donovan died in the final battle, but acknowledged his body was never recovered.

Greg put the book down when he finished the chapter and wondered if he would meet a similar end. His mind filled with worry, and he doubted sleep would come easily. However, it did, and he slept soundly until a soft knock on his door awakened him.

"Come in," Greg said groggily.

The door opened, and Molina stuck her head in.

"You must come quickly," she said and closed the door.

"What happened?" Greg asked, but Molina was already gone.

He put on his clothes and went out into the hall. Something about the hallway looked different. Just then, Fawn opened her door and joined him.

"Ready?"

"I guess so," he said.

Fawn led them down the hall. This time the hall led to a set of stairs that went down into a darker room.

Molina appeared at the base of the stairs holding a candle.

"Hurry," she urged them.

Suddenly from outside Greg heard the sound of many horns.

"The Denza," Fawn said. "They dare attack?"

Greg and Fawn hurried down the stairs and followed Molina to the far side of the dark room. She moved a stone that appeared to be part of the fireplace, and the entire fireplace slid out into the room exposing a dark tunnel. She led them into the tunnel, and then moved another rock and the fireplace slid back into place.

"This way," she instructed, turned, and led them deeper into the tunnel. They had not gone far when the tunnel divided into three separate tunnels.

Molina stopped, and rather than lead them into any of the three choices, she waved her candle into the air while looking upward. A ladder was lowered from a ledge above them.

They each climbed the ladder to the opening of a narrow tunnel that was impossible to see from below. A man whom Greg had not previously seen was waiting for them. He lit a candle of his own and the four individuals walked quickly for almost a minute until they came to the end of the tunnel.

The man stepped aside and Molina knocked on the side of the tunnel with something metal that she had drawn from a pocket in her apron. Suddenly a section of the wall opened like a door. The four entered.

"Welcome, Princess, to my little hideaway. And you, too, Gregory." The prophet greeted them with a smile.

Greg noticed a man dressed in a dark cloak shut the door and bar it from the inside. A dozen other men and women were huddled around the large room. Some were sitting at a table and others stood talking in small groups. None seemed to have interest in his or Fawn's presence, and no one showed much concern over what might be happening outside. A few candles were lit on the tables, but the room seemed to getting most of its light from some other source Greg couldn't identify.

"What is happening, Old Prophet?" Fawn asked.

"The unthinkable," he said. "The Denza have attacked my property, and at this moment are threatening my home."

"I thought you said they wouldn't," Greg stated. "What about the Zeon?"

"I did not think they would, but last night my dream of fire and death became much clearer. I am fortunate that the borders to my land have always been honored by the Zeon as separate tribal land. As you may know, it is very rare that they protect individual property. They will fight, and despite being vastly outnumbered, I believe the Zeon will repulse the attackers. However, my property is not vast. I imagine the Denza have calculated that while they may take many casualties, if they focus their attack toward getting into my house and ultimately to you, Princess, then the losses would be worth it."

"The demons," Fawn hissed. "They will destroy your beautiful home."

"If I am correct, they are burning it to the ground as we speak."

"I am sorry," Fawn said.

"Me, too," Greg added. "Do you think they will stick around to look for our bodies?"

"Not for long, at least not here at my home. The Zeon are ferocious, and it would make more sense that once the Denza believe there is no escape from the fire, they will retreat outside my borders."

"Won't the Zeon hunt them down?"

"I do not believe they will chase them too far past my borders. The Denza will have already posted lookouts around my land to see if any of us survived the attack."

"How will we escape?" Greg asked.

"I have a plan that should work, but we must go while the fighting still rages."

"We are ready," Fawn said.

Greg doubted if he was, but he kept his fears to himself.

Molina appeared carrying two mugs full of a foamy liquid. She offered one to Fawn first. She took it and drank the entire contents down. Molina turned to Greg and offered the other mug.

Greg looked at Fawn, who smiled and nodded to him. He

took the mug and took a sip. Despite the liquid's appearance, it had no flavor. Just like water, he thought. He gulped down the remaining liquid and handed the cup back to Molina. Suddenly his stomach started to expand and felt very uncomfortable.

Fawn noticed his expression. "Do not worry, Gregory, the sensation passes quickly. The little bubbles carry their own nourishment."

"We must go," the prophet stated. Led by two men with candles and followed by two others with candles, the three of them walked to the end of the room and into another tunnel.

They had not gone far when Greg spotted a ray of light hitting the side of the tunnel a little ahead of them. As they approached the spot, Greg thought he could hear muffled sounds. The group stopped just short of the beam of light.

"Gregory, there is a small break in the rocks that lets in the sunlight. If you crawl in close to it, you can see what is happening outside. It is hard for me to squeeze into that space, and I would rather not have the Princess do it."

"Sure," Greg answered, already curious to observe what was going on.

Greg had to climb onto a small shelf and then crawl into a narrow cavity in the wall of the tunnel that appeared to have been man-made. The brightness of the morning sun outside made it hard to see at first. After a few seconds, though, his eyes adjusted.

The first thing Greg realized was that he was looking out the side of a hill. The prophet's house sat clearly in the center of his view. However, it took a second or two for him to actually comprehend the activity that unfolded before him. Dozens of men, the Denza he believed, appeared to be attacking the house with bows and arrows. The tip of the arrows burned fiercely and started small fires wherever they landed in the house. Two of the attackers had reached the front door and were trying to break through.

At the same time, twenty to thirty Zeon appeared to be in the midst of the attackers. Many had one or more arrows in them, but they relentlessly pounced on the Denza. When a Zeon got a grip on a Denza it quickly threw him against nearby trees or large rocks. Greg saw many more lifeless Denza forms lying about than Zeon, but he saw enough dead Zeons to know they were not invincible. Another wave of Denza came out of the forest and charged into the open field that bordered the prophet's front yard.

One Zeon seemed to appear out of nowhere and pounced on the two Denza trying to break through the front door. He grabbed one in each hand and smashed them repeatedly against the ground. Three more Denza reached the front door and attacked the Zeon. Another volley of flaming arrows landed around them, and Greg noticed the house started to catch fire.

Caught up in what he was seeing, Greg finally recognized that the sounds he had been hearing were screams of agony and deep growling sounds.

"We better keep moving, Gregory," the prophet called to him.

Greg hurried back to the rest.

"Your home is burning. I'm sorry if we brought this trouble to you."

"Ha! You didn't bring this trouble. It has been here growing for decades in front of our own eyes. Other than Princess Fawn's brave effort, we have been content doing nothing. Your arrival may save us from ourselves. It is time the rest of the tribes open their eyes. Once you have safely escaped, and the fighting here has ended, I will make my own voyage to talk to the king."

They walked for another thirty minutes before the small group came to a spot where the tunnel simply stopped. By now, Greg had seen enough not to ask, "What now?" He knew there had to be another secret passage.

The two men up front moved to a large boulder that first appeared to be just part of the wall. They pulled it back towards them and then pushed it against the wall on the opposite side of the tunnel. The taller of the two men jumped up on the boulder and reached high up over his head. He felt against the edge of the wall until his fingers found and then reached into a hole that was just barely visible from where they were standing.

Greg heard a click and then a mechanism sliding from somewhere behind the wall where the man stood. The man jumped down off the stone, and the side of the passageway above the boulder swung inward toward Greg. Dull sunlight invaded the tunnel. The man climbed up and through the concealed exit.

Greg moved to the opening and saw thick vegetation blocking the view to the outside. Another one of his escorts climbed onto the boulder and disappeared to the other side of the leaves. The first man suddenly reappeared and nodded at the prophet.

"It is safe. Follow me," the prophet instructed.

Fawn followed the prophet, and Greg followed her out the small opening. The thick vegetation ran for about ten feet and consisted mostly of big leaves that easily gave way to Greg as he passed through them. Once past them, Greg discovered the group huddled together in a small clearing that was surrounded by dozens of trees and thick vegetation that stood at least six feet high.

He looked around but couldn't see anything.

"They should not see us here," Fawn said softly, "but we must stay quiet."

Greg nodded that he understood.

The two men pulled an item out of the bushes that Greg thought at first might be a raft, but when they turned it over it looked like a large water lily.

"That narrow path leads to a small river. You will need to conceal yourselves under this and float down the river. It is the only way you can get past the Denza. You will be safe. When I built it long ago, I did not understand why I was supposed to do it. I see now. The design is built to support two people, and it has two breathing tubes. There are also goggles that you can wear to help you see and navigate through the water."

"When will we know when it is safe to go to shore?"

"You must go well past the turn where the river joins its smaller sister. The further the better, but do not get too close to the River Yung."

"Okay," Fawn said, and the group started moving toward a narrow path at the far side of the clearing.

Everyone but Greg, that is. For the first time, he felt overwhelmed. The visions of the Denza and Zeon fighting brought reality to everything. What if the Denza saw them?

Fawn noticed his hesitation and returned to him. "I do not believe I can do this without you, Gregory."

He stared into her eyes, and for a moment, the sight of the magical coin crossed his mind. The coin had had his name on it. This was his mission.

"I'm coming," he said, and once again, with hands clasped, the two marched forward.

They had barely entered the path when Greg stepped into the river. After another few steps the water was knee high and they reached the point where the vegetation thinned out.

"Is this the same river where we saw the Zeon fishing?" Greg asked Fawn.

"No, it is the next one. We will go down this one, and it will join its little sister when we turn toward the Yung."

Greg saw a lot of holes in her explanation but decided to accept her answer. Two men held the man-made lily a couple of feet above the water, and the prophet motioned them to crawl under it. They both put their goggles in place and began to move towards the raft.

"Go with peace and be brave," he said as Greg and Fawn crawled through the water.

CHAPTER 12

Greg saw for the first time that the underside of the lily was designed much like the hang gliders he had seen on earth. He found a thick strap that went under his chest and two loops behind him that he could put his feet through while he lay under the raft, his stomach facing toward the bottom of the river. A piece of bamboo looking wood crossed in front of him as part of the frame and gave him something to hold onto.

The two men started lowering the lily before Greg located the breathing tube. He looked over at Fawn and saw she had removed a sponge-like item from the underside of the lily. He watched her place it against her mouth and nose. As it made contact with her, the sponge spread out and covered the lower half of her face. A narrow tube connected it to the top of the lily.

Without thinking twice, Greg grabbed at a similar item by his head and pressed it against his mouth and nose. Even the sensation of his body being submerged in the murky water couldn't hide the weird feeling of the sponge sealing itself against his face. At first he held his breath, fearing that if he breathed in water would shoot into his lungs. He looked at Fawn and saw that she appeared to be relaxed as she tinkered with her chest strap.

Hesitantly, Greg breathed a little air out. It felt natural, and no bubbles shot out into the water around him. Prepared to stop at the first taste of water in his mouth, he slowly inhaled. Nothing but air entered his mouth. Fascinating, he thought.

The men pushed them away from the thick vegetation. Greg felt the current of the river try to take hold of them. He looked around but the legs of their escorts could no longer be seen. The lily bumped into a patch of reeds and came to a stop. Instinctively he reached down to the river bottom, and by pulling and pushing against anything firm he could find, he maneuvered the lily past the reeds. Fawn tried to help but her arms couldn't quite reach the bottom. Connected as they were to their mobile hiding place, Greg couldn't use any of his swimming strokes to move the lily along, although a partial dog paddle seemed to help with his steering.

The current slowly drew them out into the main part of the river and away from the vegetation that bordered its banks. The water became clearer and Greg saw that the river was full of small colorful fish. He estimated that the river bottom deepened to about ten feet before it leveled off. Besides moving along with the current, the lily developed a very slow spinning motion.

They had only floated for a few minutes when he felt Fawn tap his arm. He turned to her, and she pointed at a pair of human legs standing, knee deep in the water, about fifteen feet away. Fortunately, from the position of the feet, Greg saw that the man was facing away from them. Both of them watched the legs intently until the current took them too far away to see them.

Barely five minutes later he saw three sets of men's legs rush into the river behind them but way too close for comfort. He tapped Fawn's arm, but couldn't take his eyes off the legs. Had the Denza seen through the ruse and spotted them?

All of a sudden a pair of brown hairy legs landed in the

middle of the three and one man's legs disappeared out of the water. Greg thought he could hear muffled screaming. The legs intertwined and moved away from them. A tangle of Denza and Zeon bodies crashed into the water and rolled over and over. Greg and Fawn drifted further down the river and away from the fight. Greg strained to watch, but they moved too far away. He thought he saw the river turning red around the thrashing bodies just as the vision faded from view.

He looked over at Fawn and saw her focus her eyes ahead of them. He thought he saw panic in her eyes, but when he looked forward he didn't see anything, at first. Then, in a flash, two large scaly things shot straight at them.

"Crocodiles!" Greg almost screamed the words out, but the sponge mask turned it into a muffled gasp.

As fast as they appeared, the two shot past them heading to where Greg thought the Denza and Zeon fought in the water. Instinctively, Greg reached to undo his chest strap. He needed to get to shore. He had the strap partially undone, when he felt Fawn take hold of his hand. He looked at her. She shook her head at him.

He let go of his chest strap, and she reached over and fastened it.

Greg stayed alert for other crocodiles, but in the next fifteen or so minutes, he saw nothing larger than a few trout-sized fish. He wondered if the crocodiles had sensed the blood in the water and had responded to the scent. He took some relief in the fact that they shot right by Fawn and him. They had looked similar to the crocodiles he had seen on television, but he thought they had a lot more teeth in their mouths. Maybe that had only been his imagination.

The river had gotten deeper, and Greg could no longer see the river bottom with any clarity. The water started to get warmer. Streams of bubbles drifting up from the bottom of the river appeared in front of them. Soon the bubbles were everywhere, and the water once again turned murky. An underground spring must be feeding into the river, he thought.

Something large and dark swam by below them and Greg instinctively tried to shrink himself. He wished he had his own swimming goggles. The ones they had given him did not seem to be as good as his own, and he hated not being able to see very far.

Whatever it was that swam by did not reappear, and before long they had passed through the last of the bubbles. The water became clearer, and it felt like they were moving a little faster. Fawn pointed ahead of them. Greg strained his eyes and saw that the river started its turn. Then he realized that not only was the river turning to their right, they had reached the point where it met up with the other river flowing in from their left.

The closer they got to the merge point, the quicker the current became. Soon the two rivers were one, and they were speeding along. It shouldn't be long before it would be safe to get out of the water, he thought. He wondered how Fawn would know when it was safe. He looked over at her and saw that she was watching a school of brightly colored fish swim next to them.

He noticed that several other lily pads had joined them in their journey down the river. That would help their camouflage. From anyone looking from shore, they would appear to be just one of many lily pads convoying down the river.

They continued to float for so long that the strap across Greg's chest began to irritate him. He tapped Fawn's arm to signal he wanted to get out of the water only to see that she had fallen asleep. She looked up with a start. He signaled to her that he wanted for them to go to shore, and she nodded. She also looked a little nervous, but as Greg couldn't see anything he didn't understand why.

He watched Fawn unfasten her chest strap and peel the sponge off her face. She then swam down and away from their hiding place. Greg repeated her actions and grimaced when it felt like the sponge took a layer of skin off with it when he pulled it off.

"Hurry, Gregory," Fawn shouted at him as his head popped above the water. "We are too close to it." She turned and started swimming towards shore.

Greg followed her without first looking around. Her comments made no sense to him as the shore on both sides were further away than he thought they should have been. A much stronger swimmer than Fawn, he caught up with her in no time.

"Too close to what?"

"The falls!"

Greg looked to his left and realized that the river disappeared a couple of hundred yards away. He looked back at the shoreline and felt confident he could reach it before the current carried them to the falls. He opened his mouth to say they should be okay, when it dawned on him. If they kept the pace Fawn swam at, they might not make it.

"Hold onto my belt with one hand, and continue swimming as fast as you can."

She grabbed his belt and Greg started his freestyle stroke.

He imagined he was back in the pool racing his Dad. The more the current wanted to drag him downstream, the less he fought it and simply tried to move them toward shore. Finally, barely thirty yards from the falls, they reached shallow water and were able to stand up and stagger to dry land.

Greg's muscles were involuntarily shaking. He collapsed and lay spread out on the rocky ground. Fawn sat down next to him and brushed his hair off his face.

"My hero," she said with a shaky laugh.

After a few seconds, Greg sat up and looked over at the top of the falls.

"How high is the water fall?"

"Oh, the drop isn't that far."

"Then why were you so worried about making shore?"

"We would have survived the fall, but we would have found ourselves in the River Yung.   It never gives up what it catches, and we certainly would have perished if we fell into it."

Greg stood up and looked at his clothes. Just last night they had been washed, and now they were a mess again.

"Let's go take a look."

CHAPTER 13

They strolled down to the edge of the falls. The water dropped off only about ten feet, but he saw right away why Fawn had been concerned. He had seen the River Yung when he first arrived, but then he had been two, maybe three hundred feet above it. Staring at it this close, Greg could see the ferocity of the river. Not only did the current race by, scattered throughout the river were numerous whirlpools sucking down whatever got caught in their clutches.

"I see what you mean," Greg said, and took a step back away from the edge.

"And we are in the dry season," Fawn added. "Later when the rains come it is worse."

"How much farther do we have to go?"

"Not too far now."

"We should get going," Greg said. "If the Denza are looking in this direction, we can easily be seen here."

The two walked along the bank of the Yung until they reached the edge of another forest where they moved into the trees.

"It will be harder for them to see us in here," Fawn said. "We can stay in the forest almost all the way to my land."

"How will you get back to your land, Gregory?" She asked after they had walked in silence for a while.

"I don't know," he admitted.

"Well, if the Old Prophet was correct, Donovan must have returned to his land. He must have found a way, so you may, too."

"I hope so."

"If you must stay here, I will ask my father if he will marry us."

"What?" Greg asked. His eyes opened wide with surprise at her statement.

"You do not want to marry me, Gregory?"

"No, it's not that," he said not knowing what else to say. She stared at him anticipating a further explanation. "It's just in my land, people don't marry so young."

"Oh, I guess I can wait."

I do need to get back home, Greg thought. It was bad enough to face danger, but marriage? He hadn't even had his first real date. Where was that coin?

"Do you like me, Gregory?"

"Of course."

"I know there are prettier girls than me."

"Fawn," Greg stopped and took her hands in his. "You are the most beautiful girl I have ever seen. I really do like you. But, it's like I said before, in my world the custom is for people to wait until they're older to get married."

She smiled at him, finally satisfied that it was only some silly custom of his people that she could overcome if he had to stay in her world. Greg, mistakenly, interpreted her smile that he had put her thoughts of marriage to rest.

Greg kept screening the area around them for any sign of the Denza while they hiked through the forest. He started to get a feeling that the danger was now well behind them when the sound of wolves howling startled him.

"Wolves?"

"Yes," Fawn said. "They have caught the scent of prey."

"Us?"

"I hope not. I would rather face the Yung."

The howling sounded closer.

"Quick, up this tree," Greg instructed.

He didn't need to tell Fawn twice. She clambered up the tree in mere seconds. Greg, in comparison and despite his best efforts, moved slowly up the tree. He had barely gotten to a safe height when the wolves burst into sight. He spotted four of them. He thought they looked larger than the variety he had seen a few times at the zoo, but he had to acknowledge his eyes were mostly focused on their terrifying fangs as they snapped and snarled at a large buck they chased through the forest.

Greg could see the look of terror in the eyes of the deer as it raced by. In a few seconds both the wolves and the buck were out of sight.

"I do not believe they will catch him," Fawn said as she climbed down to Greg's spot on the tree. "The mighty buck can run all day. He should be okay."

"Then we should move on before the wolves give up and come back this way looking for slower prey."

"A very good suggestion, Gregory."

After another thirty minutes of walking fast, they reached an open field that appeared to run for about a mile before it reached another forest.

"This field will become officially ours once we get the proclamation to my people. Right now it is part of the land disputed with the Denza. We might want to wait until dark to pass through it," Fawn said.

"We would be easy to see out there, but I hate to give

anyone who may be still chasing us from behind a chance to catch up."

"That is true, Gregory. I imagine by now the Denza may have figured out we escaped their attack. If they have, they know we would travel this way."

"Are we still close to the river?"

"The Yung is less than a mile away. The field runs all the way to it, but going that way will not get us any closer to where we are headed."

"If the shoreline is similar to what it was like before, there should be enough plant life and large rocks to help conceal us while we travel to the next forest. I assume the river also goes toward that forest."

"Yes, it does. But there are other dangers along that stretch of river bank."

"Like what?" Greg asked.

"Crocodiles, giant serpents, and other animals that come to drink. Even the wolves drink from the Yung."

"Oh."

They stood there at the edge of the forest looking out across it. Greg thought it looked like the rolling prairies of Kansas. He had driven through them with his parents when they went to visit an ailing uncle.

"I think your idea is a good one, Gregory."

"But what about the dangers?"

"If we are careful and move slowly, we should see any dangers before we get to close. We can go around them."

"Fawn, we won't be able to go around any wolves we encounter."

"Let us hope there are no wolves there today."

Greg looked around and selected a sturdy limb on a nearby tree.

"Can I borrow your knife?"

She handed it to him. The limb was about six feet long and about an inch in diameter where it met the tree. He used the blade like a saw and cut a slice about a quarter inch into the limb as close to the trunk of the tree as he could. The knife was not effective as a saw, but Greg thought the shallow cut might work. He then grabbed the branch and worked it back and forth with all his strength until the limb broke from the tree.

He then cut off about a foot of the outer end of the limb. Since the limb got narrower the further out he went, this part of the job only took seconds. He studied the branch. Perfect, he thought. The narrower end, about a half inch in diameter, still felt sturdy. He sat down and started sharpening the narrow end with the knife.

"I see you are a skilled hunter," Fawn said.

"I think we should make one more, for you. They may not be effective against the Denza and their weapons, but they might help us against an animal that has thoughts about making us his dinner."

It took a few minutes for Greg to find another appropriate limb, but before very long, the two were hiking through the forest toward the River Yung, each armed with a stout spear.

CHAPTER 14

The fast moving Yung had created its own gorge through this part of the country. Greg stood at the top of a steep drop off of nearly thirty feet and looked down at the river. He remembered Fawn's comments about how the river kept whoever or whatever fell into it. He certainly didn't plan to test her claim, but he did wonder if it would really be impossible to survive its current.

Greg's plan had been a sound one. The terrain along the edge of the gorge was uneven. Right away they found a lengthy section where a cavity had formed on the edge of the gorge. They climbed down about eight feet and were able to travel for a couple hundred yards on a twenty foot wide flat stretch, with the wall of rock concealing them from anybody searching for them. Rather than climb up at the other end, the wall of rock, along with the ground level itself, came down to meet them.

Fawn pointed further down the river. "From that point at the edge of the reeds, we will have to move with more caution."

Greg saw that the ground continued its slight descent and a little more than a hundred yards away, the river widened slightly and an abundance of plant life covered the edge of the water. It appeared similar to the spot where he and Fawn first got into the smaller river that morning. Until they reached the reeds, Greg believed they could be easily spotted if someone looked in their direction.

"I suggest we run there," he said.

"Yes, I agree, but Gregory, we must stop as soon as we reach the bushes."

"Okay, let's go."

The two sprinted across the open patch of land. They started together but Fawn beat him by four strides to the bushes. She stopped suddenly, and what seemed to Greg to be effortlessly, while he almost ran over her.

"Sorry," he mumbled, grabbing her arm to steady himself as much as her.

"Look over there," she said softly.

He looked off to his left, toward the river. His eyes opened wide in shock. Barely twenty feet away were two large crocodiles. They looked like they were sleeping in the sun at the edge of the reeds.

"Luckily, we didn't run to that point," Greg said.

"And, luckily we travel away from them." She started slowly walking away from the crocodiles.

The ground consisted mostly of dry sand. The various plants helped hide them, and they stayed within a couple feet of the outer edge of whatever vegetation they found themselves in. Greg realized they were walking in a large semicircle. He guessed the river expanded in this low area and formed a small shallow lake. During the rainy season, the water probably spread out and covered much more of this area. He could hear the water brush against the shoreline nearby. While staying just inside the outer edge did help conceal them from Denza scouts and spies, it made it imperative that they travel cautiously with an eye out for crocodiles and other dangers.

"Stop," Greg whispered and crouched down. Fawn, a step behind him did the same.

He saw the shadow of movement somewhere ahead. He strained to get a better view. Fawn's face appeared near his, her eyes peering through the vegetation. The proximity of her face inexplicably took his mind off the danger. She really was the prettiest girl he had ever met, he thought.

Her serious look suddenly gave way to a big smile. "It is just two Zeon."

"Will they help us get to your land?"

"No, but they pose no threat to us."

Her face remained close to his. He started to blush as she looked at him.

"Why are you staring at me?" she asked.

Greg stood up, flustered, "We need to keep going."

He didn't see her smile, and she wondered if he realized that she was just teasing him.

They walked for another twenty minutes without speaking. Greg could tell from the sun that they had turned back toward the river. "I still don't understand why the Zeon wouldn't have helped us. Certainly they know by now that the Denza are their enemy, too."

"It is even a mystery to us," Fawn said. "Are you hungry, Gregory?"

Greg stopped and saw Fawn pull a small bag out of a hidden pocket in her dress. She poured some berries out into her hand and offered them to him.

"Do you have enough for you to have some, too?"

"Yes, the Old Prophet gave them to me this morning to help us on our journey today."

Greg accepted the berries and tasted one. Like the rest of the food in this strange world, the berries tasted good. He tossed the rest into his mouth.

"We are very close now," she said. "We should reach safety before dark."

Greg looked up and noticed the sun had already crossed most of the sky. "I'll be glad to relax, and I look forward to meeting your family."

"They will like you."

While he told the truth about meeting her family, his thoughts quickly turned to his own family. He would rather be with them. Without thinking, he reached into his pockets and felt for his coin. He felt something and pulled it out. There in his hand sat a bright shiny coin, but it was a quarter, not another magic coin.

"What is that?"

"It's only a quarter. A coin we use for money in my world."

"May I see it?"

"Yes, you can have it," he handed the coin to her.

"I have never seen anything like this," Fawn said. "Whose picture is this?"

"George Washington."

She shook her head. "I do not know of him, but if you give me this coin I will have one of my father's skilled workers take his face off the coin and put your face on in its place."

"You can have it," Greg repeated.

"In exchange, you must have one of these." Fawn effortlessly pulled a ruby-like gemstone the size of a grape off one of her bracelets and gave it to him.

"But this is too expensive," he protested.

"No other Cheerakoo will have a coin like this. Many have such gemstones. I am the winner in this trade."

The ruby sparkled in his hands. He put it in the same pocket from which he had removed the coin.

"Why did that gem come off so easily from your bracelet? I would think it would have been glued on."

"You can get bracelets with the stones glued on, but then you cannot change their positions or replace them with other gems. My band is treated to attract the stones, once they are close."

"Like a magnet?"

"Yes, I understand your meaning, but the word is new to me. To remove a stone, there is a spot on the bracelet close to each gem, that when touched allows the gem to come off with little effort."

Fawn ate her last berry.

"How is it that a word can be new to you but you understand it?" Greg asked.

"I do not know for sure, but some of your words are like that. You say them, and I understand you, but I do not remember hearing the word before."

"We should start walking again," he suggested, and the two continued on.

While they walked, he wondered about Fawn's comment that the word magnet was new to her, but that she still understood his meaning. After a few minutes, a revelation came to him. In the back of his mind, ever since he arrived in this strange land, Greg had wondered how the people here understood, spoke, and even wrote in English. Was it possible that the same magic that brought him here also enabled him to speak and read Fawn's language, and that they weren't speaking English at all?

He thought about the Introduction to Spanish class he had taken in school. In that class, he knew when he said a Spanish word, or when someone said something in Spanish to him. He knew the words weren't English. Here, the language sounded natural to him, like he grew up speaking it. It felt like English, but was it? Since his arrival, he had said a few basic words that a first grader would know back home know that Fawn and the prophet had appeared to understand even though they didn't recognize the word.

Greg had already accepted what he would have believed impossible a few days ago: that the coin had somehow transported him to another world, or perhaps into another dimension. He guessed he could also believe that the coin had somehow enabled him to communicate with the people here. That there might be a few glitches in the system made it seem even more believable.

"Fawn, do all the people here speak the same language?"

"For the most part. There are some dialects that have their own accents and a few of their own words."

Greg's feet struck shallow water. "I guess it's time to head back out into the open," he said.

"Yes. We have been lucky to have made it through without running into more crocodiles."

They both stuck their heads out of the thick vegetation and looked toward the forest, now looming closer than ever.

"I think we're almost there," Greg said.

"Yes," Fawn reached over and squeezed Greg's hand again.

"Will your people be watching for you?

"Some might be, but my father insisted on secrecy. He was concerned that the Denza might find out what I was doing, so very few people were informed of my true mission."

"That makes sense. Still, your family must be worried."

Fawn nodded but didn't respond.

"When I left, Shariba, my mother's friend traveled with me. Everyone thought we went to buy fine cloth for our families. That is something we normally do every few years."

"What happened to Shariba?"

"I do not know. I am worried for her. The day I visited the king, when I returned to our lodging she was gone. I waited two days, but she never returned, and no one had any information to explain her departure. I decided it would be better to return home, but I had barely travelled for half a day when the Denza began their pursuit of me. My wagon was fast, but it lost a wheel. I thought they would catch me, but then you rescued me."

"I didn't seem to have much choice," Greg said with a smile. "If I remember right, you fell into my arms."

"And I have felt very safe ever since."

"We still have another half a mile to go. Fortunately, there appears to be a number of large rocks that might help hide us for part of the way."

They sprinted the short distance to the first grouping of large boulders. They halted and listened; everything remained quiet. Among the dozens of large rocks, they moved cautiously forward. The giant boulders would help hide them from prying eyes, but at the same time, it hindered their own ability to see ahead of them. The thought of running into another giant serpent or a crocodile frightened them both. The ground had started climbing again, and Greg noticed that the river was now a foot or two below the edge of the bank.

Not until they reached the last of the large rocks did they hear anything to worry them. The sound, when it came, was close by and directly ahead of them. Greg stopped and looked back at Fawn. She came up next to him and listened. Greg heard a snarling or growling sound that came with an occasional snapping or popping sound. The latter reminded him of sticks being broken. He peered around the edge of the boulder.

"No," he whispered to himself. They had made it so far.

Two large wolves crouched over a carcass of an animal. They had already devoured most of their unrecognizable victim.

"They are preoccupied with their dinner," Fawn said. "If we go back a little and then go around them, they may not have any interest on us."

Greg focused on her use of the word "may" and didn't feel particularly happy with her plan.

"I don't know," he said.

"The longer we wait the worst it will be. Now they have a meal."

"Okay," Greg agreed, still not committed.

The two backtracked about thirty yards, and then started slowly out into the open field.

"I do not think we should run. It will only attract the wolves," Fawn said.

"Okay, but out here we are in the open. The Denza will certainly see us if they are watching."

"I am sure they are, but we only have to get to the forest."

Greg looked ahead. He estimated that he could run to the forest in three minutes. An almost irresistible urge to run seized him. The sound of a nearby growl brought about the exact opposite effect. He froze.

In their focus on the two wolves at the carcass, they had not seen the third wolf. The alpha wolf, Greg thought. A huge wolf, its muzzle shone red with blood. He must have eaten first and moved to the shade of the boulders to rest. Their departure from the rocks took them too close to him.

"Keep walking away from him," Fawn said.

Greg forced himself to move. His knees felt like jelly.

The wolf stood glaring at them, but did not attack.

They took about a dozen steps, and Greg made the mistake of beginning to feel safe, when the wolf began to walk slowly after them.

"Not good," Greg whispered. He glanced over at the two wolves. Their focus remained with their dinner.

The wolf did not close the gap between them. He appeared to be studying them. Picking out which one if us would make the best dessert, Greg thought.

"Fawn, you keep walking. I'll stand here and keep him away from you."

"No way. I will not leave you alone with that beast."

The three continued for another thirty paces, but then the unfortunate happened. Fawn, like Greg had kept her eyes focused on the wolf. She didn't see a small hole in the ground and stepped right into it. She tripped and fell. The sudden movement resulted in the wolf's instinctive charge.

Fawn jumped back up and was on her feet seconds before the lone wolf reached them. They both stood, side by side, with their spears pointed straight at the charging beast. Their audacity must have surprised the wolf, because it suddenly stopped just outside the reach of the spears.

"Arghh!" Greg yelled and taking a step forward, jabbed at the wolf. The end of the spear struck the wolf's snout, and the wolf backed away a few steps.

Fawn and Greg took a few, slow steps backwards to increase the distance between them and the wolf. For a moment the three stared at each other. Then, as suddenly as it had come after them, the wolf turned around and trotted away.

"A good thing he had already eaten today," Greg said softly, mostly to himself.

The two resumed their slow walk away from the wolves, but they kept a close eye on all three of the beasts.

"Look," Fawn whispered and pointed to the right of them away from the river. Three Denza walked at the edge of the forest that Fawn had identified as their goal. "I do not think they have seen us. We should go closer to the river's edge."

They started moving parallel to the forest ahead of them, toward the River Yung and away from the three Denza they had spotted in the distance. Once they reached the point where the ground stopped and dropped nearly fifteen feet down to the river, they found a small depression in which they did their best to hide. Forced to lie down to take advantage of the foot and a half deep depression that barely concealed the two of them, Greg asked the obvious question first.

"Do you think they spotted us?"

"They must not have, or they would have attacked."

"How many did you see?"

"Three."

"Same here," Greg agreed. "What would they be doing in your land?"

"If they behave peacefully, we do not mind them or anyone else on our land. We know they disputed our ownership of the vast lands that the king has now proclaimed are in fact ours. There have even been a few minor skirmishes, but they would not cause any trouble in the lands that even they acknowledge are ours."

"And, that's the land in the forest and beyond?"

"Yes," Fawn said.

"We are close. I'm sure we'll reach the forest."

"Once we do, I shall ask my father to put on a big feast to honor you."

"I am getting hungry," Greg said with a grin.

"Think we can reach that large rock without being seen?" Fawn asked.

Greg peered out above the edge of the depression. A few bowling ball sized rocks partially blocked his view.

"I don't see anything."

"If we can reach that rock safely, there is a narrow ledge that runs along the wall about half way down to the river that we can take the rest of the way."

"Is it dangerous?"

"No, when I was younger I played along that ledge. Of course my parents never knew I did so, but it is safe. There is also a small cave right below that rock, so no one can see you from above."

"Sounds like the way to go," Greg acknowledged.

Fawn picked her head up and peered over the edge. "I do not see anything either. Should we go?"

"Okay."

CHAPTER 15

They both tried to stay low and run at the same time toward the giant rock. They had barely reached the rock when three arrows struck the ground around them. They stopped behind the rock. Another arrow sailed overhead.

"I can't believe it," Greg shouted. "We're almost there."

"Where did the arrows come from? We may still have time to reach the ledge. We will be safe there."

Greg took a quick glance around the edge of the rock. He still couldn't see anyone.

"Where are they?" he said.

"Come on," Fawn said and ran to the cliff. Just as she reached the edge an arrow blazed down and scratched her arm as it went by. She instinctively dropped to the ground.

Greg ran out to her side and lied down next to her.

"Are you okay?"

"Yes, barely a scratch."

He looked over the edge. "I see the ledge. It'll be easy to reach."

The cliff wall dropped fairly straight to the water below. The river was only fifteen feet below them. Like the section of riverbank they had hiked earlier that day, the force of the water had eroded away everything but solid rock. The narrow ledge, made from solid rock, stuck out barely eight feet below.

"I don't see the cave."

"You cannot see it from here, but it is there."

"Look!" Greg shouted.

Three Denza, probably the ones they saw earlier, had broken from the cover of the trees and were running diagonally in front of them. They ran toward the river as well as toward them.

"They are trying to cut us off. We should go," Fawn urged.

"They'll reach the river's edge before we can reach the forest. We'll be sitting ducks down there."

"But we cannot go back!"

"Wait, I have a plan, but we must be quick!" Greg instructed. In the next few seconds, he outlined his thoughts.

"I do not like it! It is too dangerous for you." Fawn exclaimed, but she, too, knew it was their best chance.

Their three attackers approached the river's edge and turned their charge directly at them. They were still nearly two hundred yards away. One of the three put a horn to his lips and blew into it. The same ominous sound that Greg had heard earlier now echoed through the valley.

Fawn stood up and staggered, the arrow that had barely scratched her now clasped tightly under her armpit. Greg hoped the Denza would believe the arrow had struck Fawn in the chest. He jumped up to her and pretended to pull at her to get her away from the cliff. She pushed him away and turned so the Denza couldn't help but see what happened next.

She reached into the folds of her clothing and pulled out the bright colored tube that held the king's proclamation. In what almost seemed like slow motion to Greg, Fawn turned slightly back toward him and tossed the tube to him. He caught it and looked at the rapidly approaching enemy. They had to have seen what happened.

The dangerous part of the plan came next. Fawn stumbled

backwards and tumbled over the cliff. Greg fought the urge to go to the edge and look for her. If everything worked according to plan, he wouldn't see her anyway. Besides it was time for him to run.

He spun around and sprinted away from the approaching Denza. He fought the urge to look back, knowing that it would just slow him down. After running a couple hundred yards, though, he could no longer fight the urge.

The three Denza were standing at the edge of the cliff looking down. Greg stopped. He had extended the distance between them and felt it safe to pause, since they had also stopped. No doubt they were suspicious, he thought.

His rest was short lived. The three Denza looked at him and resumed their chase.

"Suckers," Greg said to himself. He started to turn and run when he saw an amazing sight. A large group of Zeon emerged from the forest and converged on the general area where Fawn said the ledge would have taken them. They must have known she was returning and were there now to protect her.

He also saw her suddenly emerge onto the cliff wall and run along the narrow ledge toward the Zeon and safety. As if she knew he was watching her, Fawn suddenly stopped and waved back at him. She would be safe now, the proclamation still with her in one of her many hidden pockets. He gave her a "thumbs up". Quite a distance separated them, but with her vision Greg knew she saw it.

No more time to waste, he said to himself and once again started his run.

The plan had worked. At least, the first half of the plan had. Fawn would be safe and the land that the Cheerakoo claimed would now be legitimatized. The Denza's plan to ultimately rule the kingdom was stopped – at least for now, and maybe forever.

However, Greg still had the second half of the plan to worry about: his own escape. He had a hundred yards on his chasers, but he didn't know how fast they could run, or how long they would chase him. He tossed the small tube that had once held the proclamation up in the air. It landed behind him, and he hoped the Denza would stop and inspect the tube. If they did, he thought they might stop chasing him. The tube contained nothing and should be enough of a hint to let the Denza realize they had been tricked. It would be too late for them to go back and find Fawn.

Greg turned away from the river and away from the last spot he had seen the wolves. He would run around the mostly dry lake bed retracing the steps they had taken earlier. Glancing back he saw the Denza stop and inspect the empty tube. He slowed to conserve strength.

The Denza seemed to be arguing among themselves. One pointed back toward the Cheerakoo's forest. All three appeared angry. They turned their focus toward Greg, and the one with the horn blew it again. This time, Greg heard another horn respond in the distance. The three Denza reinitiated their pursuit.

"Darn," Greg said to himself as he sprinted to the far side of the reeds. He looked around as he ran, but he didn't see any other Denza. He had increased the distance between himself and his three pursuers.

He thought about ducking into the thick water plants to hide. He ran close to the edge of the reeds, using them as cover.

The Denza couldn't see him now, but if he did stop and hide, they would surely look for him. They might even kill him if they found him. Better to keep running, he thought. The river started to get closer and Greg was just about to turn away from the reeds when a large hand shot out of the bushes, and he was violently yanked into them.

He looked into the face of a Zeon, only inches away from his own.

"Be silent, you will be safe with us."

CHAPTER 16

Too shocked to say anything, Greg remained silent as the Zeon literally carried him a few yards deeper into the thick vegetation. A second Zeon appeared. The two he and Fawn had seen earlier that same day, he thought.

The second Zeon held a large fish, maybe a yard long, in one of his hands. It looked heavy, but the Zeon carried it like it was a big feather. He suddenly walked off in a hurry with the fish. He moved quietly through the vegetation, but Greg thought he stopped about ten yards from them.

The muffled sound of men talking came into range.

"Where did he go?" one asked.

"On to those rocks ahead," a second voice answered.

"Maybe into the reeds," the third Denza responded.

Suddenly a loud commotion broke out nearby. The sound of large creatures thrashing about, and giant jaws smacking shut disturbed the relative calm.

"The crocodiles have him," one of the Denza shouted.

"Go see," ordered one of the men.

"You go see. I'm not going in there," said a second.

"I will check it out," said another.

The second Zeon silently reappeared without the fish. The first Zeon again picked Greg up by one arm, and they all moved deeper into the marsh. Greg wanted to yell at the Zeon and say that he was hurting him, but instead he grimaced and remained silent. He certainly didn't want the Denza to know where he was.

The sound of the crocodiles fighting over the snack that the Zeon had tossed to them, to fool the Denza, concealed any noise the Zeon may have caused as they moved another eight or nine steps deeper into the vegetation.   Greg saw a six foot snake slither out of the way of the Zeon.

The three stopped at a small spot where the vegetation had thinned out and an old, moss covered tree trunk lay across the ground.

"We shall stay here for now," whispered the first Zeon.

"How is it that I can understand you?" Greg asked softly.

"You are not of this world, are you?"

"No."

The shouts of one of the Denza interrupted them.

"The crocodiles had something, but they had already eaten it by the time I could see them. I saw blood on a few bushes, but that was all."

"Maybe they solved our problem for us," another of the Denza said.

"Only if that was him and if he had the king's proclamation."

"Chaka, did you get her?" It sounded like more Denza had arrived.

"We are not sure, my Prince."

"What do you mean?"

"We struck the young princess with an arrow and she fell into the River Yung. Before she fell, we saw her give the royal container to the strange young man with her. We chased him here, and we believe his attempt to hide was interrupted by the crocodiles."

"Believe?"

"We saw him come around the reeds, but lost sight of him briefly. When we arrived here, the crocodiles had just caught something. By the time we reached the crocodiles, there was nothing left to see."

"Could he have gone on further?"

"It is possible, but I think we would have seen him before he reached cover."

"If he did escape that way, that only delays his capture and takes him further away from Cheerakoo land. Before we leave this area we must do a further search."

"Yes, my Prince."

"Everyone!" a voice shouted. "Into the lake bed, find the stranger."

"Did you hear that?" Greg asked the Zeon.

"We cannot understand them."

"They are coming to look for me."

"Here," the second Zeon spoke for the first time. He leaned over and picked up one end of the big log. A hollow area had been dug out underneath it.

Greg looked at the small damp area and then back up at the Zeon.

"Hurry," said the first Zeon.

The space didn't look inviting, and Greg wondered if he could even fit into it, but the sound of many feet approaching was sufficient incentive. He crawled into the space and the Zeon lowered the log on top of him. A small knot of wood pressed into his back. Greg squirmed around to get more comfortable.

"Good thing I'm not claustrophobic," Greg thought to himself. A pile of leaves were tossed against the only gap out from which he could see. He hoped the snake he saw a few minutes before didn't come back thinking this might be a good hiding spot for him, too.

"What do we have here?" a Denza voice sounded above.

"Two of those smelly monkeys," another voice said.

Greg heard a low growl come from one of the Zeon.

"Don't irritate them," another Denza said.

"We outnumber them."

"But we are only three, right here. Those are not good odds. Let us move on and follow orders. We can tell the prince about the Zeon. If he deems it worthy, we can return to attack them with a force of ten or more. Those are better odds."

Greg could hear the footsteps of the Denza while they moved away. The Denza did not return, and just as Greg was about to ask for his freedom, the log was lifted off him.

He stood up and stretched his cramped muscles.

"Are they gone?" he asked.

"Yes they moved on."

"I was afraid they were going to attack you."

"It would not have been wise of them to do so."

"What should we do now?"

"We should wait here until dark. It will be here soon," said the first Zeon.

"We do not like the Denza," said the second Zeon.

"You shouldn't. The Old Prophet said they want to rule over the entire land, and that they want to stop your migration by closing your three migration routes."

The two Zeon looked at each other.

"The Old Prophet is wise. Like the Cheerakoo and many others, he treats us with respect. He is a friend of ours. It is too bad I cannot say the same about the Denza."

"What is your name?" Greg asked the first Zeon, the one who had grabbed his arm as he had run by.

"Milo," the Zeon replied, "and do you have one?"

"Yes, my name is Greg."

"Mine is Pala," offered the second Zeon.

"How did you know that I am not of your world?" Greg asked.

"We have many legends of off-worlders coming to Vanou to do good, and to do bad."

"Vanou?"

"This world."

Greg thought it interesting that neither Fawn nor the Old Prophet, had never mentioned a name for their world and yet, the Zeon did right away.

"More importantly, we could understand you when you talked. Word has spread about you ever since two of our kind overheard you speaking. Your strange clothing reinforced our theory about you."

"Also," the Zeon named Pala spoke, "we learned from the old man that he was waiting for an off-worlder."

"I thought you couldn't talk to the people of this planet."

"That is correct, but we have a strange relationship with the old man you visited on your journey here. Even though we don't understand his speech, we often understand what he is trying to say or ask. We believe he sometimes understands us, too."

"Did the Denza succeed in burning down his home?"

"Yes."

"That is too bad," Greg said.

"Yes, but he will rebuild."

"Then he is okay?"

"Yes, he has not been harmed."

"Good." Greg thought for a moment and then spoke again, "many of your kind were killed by the Denza when they attacked the prophet's home. I do not understand why you fight so fiercely to protect someone else's land, but ignore the same people the next day when you see them?"

"It is the way we are. The way we have been for a thousand years. It has been our sworn duty for so long I am not sure even we understand it."

"There are people in this world, like the Cheerakoo, who consider you their friends, but there are others, the Denza, who seek to destroy you so they can rule this kingdom."

The two Zeon again looked at each other.

"I believe the Denza wanted to stop Princess Fawn from getting back to her people, because she is carrying with her the king's proclamation that acknowledges that much of this land we are now in is their rightful land. If they had succeeded, the Denza would move to take over more of the open lands until they could put a choke hold on many of the smaller tribes and control your migratory routes."

"Are you sure of this?" Milo asked.

Greg thought for a second. After all, what he just said he had heard from the Old Prophet who had espoused it as a theory, not a fact.

"Yes, I am." Somehow, Greg knew that imparting this message between the people of this world and the Zeon was part of his purpose in coming here.

"The young Cheerakoo female, Princess Fawn," Pala said the

name slowly like he had heard it for the first time, "was carrying this proclamation?"

"Yes."

Pala looked at Milo. Some silent message seemed to pass between them, and Pala stood up and trotted off.

"He went to ensure the Princess is safe."

"I think she is, but I would like to know, too."

"You asked why we protect certain territories. A thousand years ago Vanou was self-destructing with wars among all men and even between the species. It had been going on for as long as anyone remembered."

"That sounds terrible."

"It was barbaric. Fortunately, this vast continent was discovered and thousands fled from the violence and the warfare. Many who came here were Zeon. There are only a few safe ways to travel into this land from the outside world. Those that reached this sanctuary settled in their own small portions of the countryside, and for the most part, ignored or tolerated the people of other tribes."

"Then what happened to start the war here?" Greg asked.

"It didn't start here. The war came here when the last of the powerful warlords, the leader of the Banjai, discovered this place and attacked it. By then, the rest of the world had become mostly wasteland. Entire civilizations had been decimated. Entire races of people and species of animals were wiped out."

"That's terrible."

"It started slowly here. First, a small troop of Banjai found one of the passes and entered our land. They immediately attacked the first settlement they encountered. After the attack, they left with whatever they had stolen. They also took prisoners to turn into slaves."

"I guess you knew then that your world was no longer safe."

"Yes, all the tribes united, even the Zeon. The first time that had ever happened."

"Could the Zeon communicate with the people back then?" Greg asked.

"No. But we understood what had happened, and we knew what we had to do. A small probing attack occurred shortly after the first and was repulsed. The Banjai didn't press a full attack for nearly two years. When they did a great battle ensued. We Zeon believe the fate of our entire world rested in the outcome of that horrific war."

"Obviously it turned out okay."

"Yes. An off-worlder like yourself came and helped turn the tide. At our darkest point, he organized a counter attack that destroyed the enemy. Only a handful of Banjai escaped. His ability to speak to both the people and to the Zeon enabled them to coordinate their battle plans."

"Donovan."

"Yes, so you have heard of him."

"Yes. The prophet mentioned him."

"He is also responsible for our behavior in protecting the tribes' lands."

"How so?"

"He fought the last battle against the fleeing Banjai with the Zeon. The war had been won by then but no one wanted the Banjai to escape with any kind of a force that could reorganize and return later. After the victory, Donovan sat with our council of elders. He explained to them the importance of the Zeon in this world."

"This world would not be the same without the Zeon."

"You are right, Greg. We are a peaceful race. While we can be fierce, we are content with what we have. Donovan understood that, but more importantly, he appreciated our intelligence. He explained to us that in order for our new world to remain peaceful we had to ensure the integrity of the tribes' lands by protecting those lands from the other tribes when needed. He knew that the "mellow stone", the blue gem that the tribes' use to delineate their borders, has a strange effect on us."

"Once it's activated on their public maps, you can somehow sense the boundaries. Is that correct?"

"Yes. Donovan had already explained to the people how vital it was to have public maps for all to see and to use the mellow stone. He had risked his life to save the Zeon from the Banjai. He could speak to both the tribes and to us. We knew he spoke with wisdom. Over the generations his guidance has kept war from our lands."

"And now the Denza want to change it all."

"It appears so," said Milo.

"She is safe and with her people," Pala said. His sudden, quiet reappearance surprised Greg.

"Great," Greg said.

"Pala, we must advise the council about the Denza's intentions."

"But our role is not to interfere unless another's land is being violated."

"True, but all Zeon must understand the threat posed by the Denza. We must be vigilant. The attack against us at the old man's home was the first like that in many years. We must understand that wasn't simply a mistake but part of a larger plan. We must remain vigilant, more so now than ever."

"Yes," Pala agreed.

CHAPTER 17

"Do you want to go see the girl?" Pala asked.

"I'd love to see Princess Fawn again, but I feel that I must return to my home now. Unfortunately, I'm not sure how."

"Our history says that my ancestors took Donovan back to where he came from."

"Back to earth?"

"I think it simply means they took him back to the location where he first came to our world. From that point, Donovan travelled back to his world alone. I have never heard that any Zeon went with him."

"I wonder…" Greg said to himself. Could it be that easy?

"Do you want to go there?" Pala asked.

"Yes, but I'm not sure how to get back there."

"We heard you came from the great cat's cave. That feat alone made you something special among the Zeon."

"Why is that?"

"To us, the cave of the great cat is a special place. We dare not enter it," Milo said.

"The few foolish Zeon who have dared to try ended up as dinner for the great cat," Pala elaborated.

"I could go to the other end."

The two Zeon looked at each other. "We do not know where the other end is."

Greg remembered that the entrance was hidden by the water fall. He doubted if he could find it himself.

"If we waited until the cat left the area, I could get in."

"Getting in is the easy part. Getting back out is the challenge."

"Still, for some reason I can't explain, I feel that I must go there," Greg said.

"Then we will take you there. We will leave tomorrow, as soon as the sun can be seen."

"Where will we sleep tonight?" Greg asked. Darkness had settled in around them.

"Here."

Greg looked around. Nothing looked very comfortable. It would be a long night, he thought.

Sleep didn't come easy, and on a few occasions the sounds of the night awoke him. However, he felt safe being with the two Zeon. A furry hand gentling shaking him brought him out of his sleep. He looked up and saw a grayish pink, dawn sky. The darkness around him had not been fully chased away by the sun. At home, he would have rolled over and insisted on more sleep. Today, however, he jumped up and felt excited about the prospect of getting home.

To his surprise, at some point during the night three additional Zeon had joined them. One of the three appeared to be younger than the others. All three stared at Greg with fascination.

"You are quite the item of interest," Milo said to him. "I wouldn't be surprised if we were joined by many more before we reach our destination."

"Hello," said Greg to the new arrivals.

"Ahhh! He can talk," said the young Zeon.

"Don't mind Manga. He's still young and a bit ill mannered."

"That's okay. Manga, it's nice to meet you."

Manga looked at the older Zeon, and in an effort to show that he, too, had manners replied, "It is an honor to meet you."

The trek back to the cave began. While the journey passed without any incident with the Denza or any other wild creatures, it still turned out to be two fascinating days for Greg. More and more Zeon joined them as they made their way. Very few talked to Greg, most were content simply to hear him talk to the others.

Manga turned out to be the exception. He had dozens of questions about what it was like living on earth. He also wanted to know why Greg had come to their world.

When Greg had answered Manga's question by saying he came to help Princess Fawn, and hopefully the Zeon, Milo interrupted him.

"Manga, our friend Greg understates the importance of his visit to our world. By helping the Princess take the proclamation to her people, he enabled the new borders to be publicly displayed. This means everything to us. He also informed us of the Denza's evil desire to rule the world. Individually they are very important, but combined they may have been critical in safeguarding peace in our world and perhaps our very existence."

"Oh, Milo, I don't know if –."

"Greg," Milo interrupted. "You fail to understand. By getting the proclamation to the Cheerakoo, you succeeded in seriously blocking the Denza's efforts. That is very important, but there are other ways they could eventually achieve their goal. By informing us of the Denza's plans we have time to consider how their behavior should affect our own behavior."

"Can you change your behavior to be more active against the Denza?"

"Of course, but it won't be easy and will take time. The new Cheerakoo boundaries will give us time to agree on whatever course we choose."

Greg nodded. He thought it would take time for the Zeon change their ways. He didn't know if change would be a good thing either.

As if he could read his mind, Milo continued. "Donovan cautioned us to not get involved in the tribes' internal matters. A thousand years of behavior cannot simply be discarded."

"You will have to give this matter a lot of thought," Greg said.

"We will. The Zeon spend a lot of time debating the simplest of things. This will keep our elders busy for a long time. At least, Greg, we have been cautioned that the evil ways of long ago may be once again trying to return to our world. That is something we could not have imagined on our own."

When they passed the lands of the Old Prophet, Greg was happy to see him out working on the construction of a new house. Greg waved from a distance, and the prophet smiled and waved back.

CHAPTER 18

When they reached the mouth of the cave, which Greg knew was actually a tunnel, he noticed the saber-toothed tiger was nowhere in sight.

"We came at a good time. The great cat is down in the valley hunting. Still, it would be wise not to waste any time," said one of the Zeons.

"Thanks for bringing me back here," Greg said to his escorts.

"You will be remembered and honored forever among the Zeon," Milo said.

"Come back again," Manga told him.

"Manga, will you do me a favor?" Greg asked.

"Of course."

"Can you take this and give it to Princess Fawn? It will be something for her to remember me by." Greg handed Manga a small, two inch by three inch photo of himself with his parents and his sister that he had removed from his wallet. It had been taken only weeks before.

"He will," Milo said, "and I will go with him to help him identify the young Cheerakoo female. Now, you go home."

"Thanks again," Greg waved goodbye and headed toward the tunnel. He knew the tunnel would be dark inside, so he broke a three foot branch off a bush to take with him. The thin branch would not be a good weapon, but Greg thought in the darkness he could use it like a blind man might use a cane. He did not want to fall into another pit. The next one might prove more difficult to climb out.

The light from the entrance helped him for a good portion of his walk through the tunnel. He imagined he had traveled a third of the distance before the darkness became a problem. His walking stick came in handy as more than once he almost stepped into a hole. He heard the sound of the waterfall before he could see it. Looking back he could still see the light of the tunnel's entrance, but sufficient light didn't shine through the waterfall ahead to make it visible.

Finally, he thought he could see it. The inside of the tunnel seemed to be getting brighter, and he started jogging. The sound turned into a roar and he thought he could almost feel the spray of the water when a sense of alarm shot through his body. He stopped still.

There, it moved. He remained motionless and tried to identify the movement. Barely twenty feet in front of him, it moved again. Curled up in a small, shallow pit, positioned right next to the wall of the tunnel, was a large snake. Not as large as the one that attacked Fawn, but still, it looked big.

Greg couldn't see its head. Its body was as big around as the end of a baseball bat. He thought the snake might be asleep since it hadn't reacted to Greg's approach. He took a couple of slow steps, hugging the opposite wall of the tunnel as he did. The snake didn't move.

He couldn't go back. By now the saber tooth tiger could be there. Besides he wanted to go home. He took a few more slow steps and tried to be as light on his feet as he could. All at once something in the back of his mind screamed run, and Greg dashed for the falls. At the same moment the snake struck at him, missing him by mere inches. In the corner of his vision, Greg saw fangs that had to be six inches long snap-shut behind him.

He glanced back and saw the snake chasing him. The falls were only a few yards away, but if he stopped the snake would be all over him. He made his decision at the last second, and looking back he knew he never had another option. The snake was almost upon him. He leapt into the waterfall knowing that he would either be returned home or would perish when he struck the rocks below.

The water smacked into him, almost knocking the breath out of him. Water surrounded him, and he struggled to gain some control over his spinning and tumbling fall. Inexplicably, a hand reached into the water. Fawn? He grabbed at the hand and a flash of light blinded him.

He coughed, sputtered, and opened his eyes. He was standing in front of the small fountain in Disneyworld again. His sister Cindy, not Fawn, stood next to him.

"I'm sorry, Greg, but right after your coin went into the water, I had this irresistible urge to get it back out. I just had to." She held the coin out to him.

Confused he reached over and took it from her. It looked like the same coin, but the inscription was different. For a second the coin glowed in his hand, much like it did the very first day when he discovered it. This time, however, the glow only lasted for a few seconds. The words were different, too. This time it only read "Thank you". Greg looked down at the fountain, but he could see no other coins.

"I hope you aren't angry with me."

"Cindy, I'm not angry with you. I think you just saved my life."

She looked at him, not having any idea what he meant.

"How long have we been standing here?"

"Maybe one minute," Cindy replied.

Greg looked down at his clothes. He saw no sign of the wear and tear of the last few days. He wasn't even wet. Did he have a hallucination? Could it have all been a dream? He looked over and saw his parents. They were right where they were before he tossed the coin into the fountain.

Dream or not, he was happy to be home.

"Come on Cindy, let's head back."

"But nothing happened."

Greg thought she looked a little disappointed. Maybe nothing did happen, he thought. By chance, though, his hand brushed against his pocket and he felt something. He reached in, pulled out the gemstone Fawn had given him, and then quickly put it back into his pocket. He pulled out his wallet and looked for the small picture of his family. It wasn't there.

"Actually, Cindy, something did happen."

"What?"

"Give me some time to think about it, but I will tell you soon. I'll have to tell someone about it. Now though, I want us to have a nice time on our vacation. When we get back home, I'll tell you. And, Cindy..."

"Yes."

"It will have to be our secret."

"Okay."

"Even if you don't believe the story I tell you, it will have to be our secret."

"Sure, Greg."

He reached over and brushed the tip of her nose with his finger. She giggled, and they walked off to join their parents.

THE END

A Mouse Gate Adventure Book
What's your adventure?